Vampire's Lust

CHANTELLE P NCUBE

Published by Chantymin Media, 2022.

VAMPIRE'S LUST

First edition. June 22, 2022.

Copyright © 2022 CHANTELLE P NCUBE.

ISBN: 979-8201814632

Written by CHANTELLE P NCUBE.

Table of Contents

To all the army who Stan BTS, this is for you Borahae, I purple you….

Vampire's Lust

Falling in love is easy as they say but what do you do when you fall in love with an alpha vampire and his brothers. Who will you choose? - Chantymin Fiction

Written by:

Chantelle Primrose Ncube

<u>About the Author</u>

My name is Chantelle Primrose Ncube. I was born in Zimbabwe where I spent my early years. I am naturally an introvert and I find serene peace when I am alone. My favorite color is cyan blue, yellow, turquoise blue, and white. I love peace because it helps me gather my thoughts and makes me feel like I am breathing in a non-judgmental environment.

I grew up following BTS, they were my therapy when my mom and granddad passed away. I believe they helped me see my true potential. I was in a bad space but when I listened to any BTS song I would find myself feeling at peace and happy. Wherever I go I'm always asked how I remain happy all the time even when I am going through a hard space and all I can say is thank you BTS. I also owe everything to my grandfather who raised me in the book, he first introduced me to reading newspapers and I always was drawn to mystical, supernatural, and crime themes which led me to watch a lot of series that contained all that. As I wrote this book I had a lot of thoughts as to how the boys would be if they were vampires not idols and it got me flowing with this fantastic and mystical story.

This is a fiction book on vampires with our beloved Korean pop group BTS members, it's full of thrust but you have to read it and satisfy your desires, A girl falls in love with a vampire, he will do everything he can to protect her or will he die for her?

<u>*Dedication*</u>

To my late grandfather who taught me to never allow anyone to put me down, to go for something because that one person matters. To my army friends who have always supported me no matter what and to you reading this book, smile because you are loved and appreciated by me. I purple you all.

Chantelle p Ncube
Vampire's Lust
Volume one

Chapter 1

Do I have to go? All my life is here mom, I grin looking at her. "Yes, my dearest daughter, we have no choice or they take you away from me", she smiles at me. B-but mom it's a very creepy place and it's always so cold aiiiiisssssshhhh I can't. I look at my elder sister Rose, hoping she could save me from leaving home. Yahh, convince mom she always listens to you Rose... "Nooooooo way don't get me involved Y/n", she looked aside. B-but............ "No buts Y/n, you have to be a big girl, I'll miss you little sis, and I would have loved to come but someone gotta take care of these old folks", she smirked. "Hey, who you calling old huh?" mom scolded. "Not you hahaha, sorry mom", she smirked again. Okay, I'm ready guys, I hug them and leave with the driver, having no idea what awaits me in a new town, new people.

Y/n P.o.v

What awaits me is scary but what can I do, it's a new school, new people aiiiishh who knows how the kids will be? Will they bully me or be nice? I'm not a popular girl, just great... "Y/n, Y/n, Y/n", someone called out to me. Who's calling me? "My Y/n it's been a very long time", uncle Kai arrived making me smile happily. Hi uncle, I hug him tightly, I missed you so much. "How you doing Y/n hmm?" he asked observing every part of me. I'm ok uncle, how have you been? How is my little sister Lisa doing? "So many questions, I'm ok and you'll see Lisa soon", he laughed. Okay, Okay uncle, I put my bags on the back seat and we started the journey home. "Y/n, Y/n, I'm so happy you came, I have been so lonely." Lisa rushed hugging me not letting go. Hey dear, how have you been? She quickly hugs me again not allowing me to finish speaking. "I'm fantastic now that you're here, Are you ready for school tomorrow?" she smirked. Yeah, I guess. "Ready to meet hot guys hahaha, you know the drill Hun", she laughed looking at me naughtily. Hey stop it, I'm not after boys, but wait are they very hot? "Oh, yes they are very hot, tell you, especially these three brothers but no one is good enough for them at school. No one has ever dated them, all they do is have fun", she looked at me. Can't wait to see them but let's sleep Lisa I don't want to be late on my first day at school, goodnight, I'm just so happy to see you. "Me too, Okay, okay, but, night let's sleep then. Morning came in a hurry, I felt like I never even slept, my body was just so tired. "Are you ready for school Y/n? If anyone bothers you let me know, I run that turf", she smirked. Thanks, Lisa but that's supposed to be my line, remember I'm the older one. "Yeah, yeah but at this school, I'm older and I'm running late for class now, I love you, and try to enjoy your first day", she hugs me and leaves. Ok bye, just as I turned around my gaze is fixed on three guys and their aura was so cold yet so hot and they were handsome and all you could do is stare. Why is my heart beating so fast? Why are they such a mystery? One of them turned and looked at me, and smirked. What the hell, I closed my locker and made my way to class. The lectures were such a bore, I blended pretty well. I want to go see my friend but where Lisa is, have to tell her where I'm going. "Tell me what?" she startled me. Want to go see my friend she lives around here, so I might be a little late. "Ok Y/n, go and enjoy yourself, and by the way did anything happen today?" she smiled at me with talking lips. Yes, Hun, three guys came so hot and one of them kept staring at me. "Don't mind him, Hi I'm Taehyung but you can call me Tae and you must be Y/n?" he said looking at me. Yes I am, thanks, and nice to meet you. "You smell like a rose but see you around", he smirked as he left. Is he always like this? "Girl, they never speak to anyone you the first...I can't believe that just happened", she looked at me with a shocked expression. Yeah, I'm leaving, if I stay with you any longer, I'll go crazy.

I never get tired of this beautiful view and now I have a long journey, as I was going a car passed me by splashing a puddle on me. What the hell dude seriously * as he came out of the car I felt cold spots, his eyes were dark and brown, his hair was silky wet and he had the most handsome lips, your body was just lured to his scent. He came closer to me with his broad shoulders and he made my body feel like it could worship him. He was dark and dangerous and all I wanted was to devour his lips. "I'm sorry Luna did me get you wet?" he looked at me. I just stood there lost in his lustful eyes, brown eyes, Breathe Y/n, damn breathe, He came closer a few feet away, and I could feel his hot breath on me. How could any guy be as sexy as him huh? I asked myself that not noticing he was staring at me. "Earth to you, Are you ok?" he smirked. I'm fine thank you.....words left my brain making me feel like I was dumb. "I love your scent it's intriguing", He just leaves without saying anything. What did I just experience, my knees feel so weak, and I sat by the steps that were nearby as I felt mixed emotions. Was I falling for Mr. Dark and dangerous? Y/n get a grip have you seen yourself? He's probably taken, what is he doing to me aiiiishh I don't want this or to feel like this. "Hey, Y/n, sorry to bother you just saw you sitting by the steps and alone, Are you ok?" Tae asked. Wait, how did you find me? I'm sorry I'm fine. "That's not important Y/n, you dropped your phone so I thought of bringing it to you", he said smiling at me. You know you could have given me at school tomorrow. "Nah I won't be there tomorrow, going on a hunting trip with family", he smirked. Oh, that's great. "Take a walk with me, I'm bored please, and I can show you places you haven't seen before", he smirked again. Sure ok, as long it's a safe place, but bare this in mind I know how to hit, I smile.

"I won't I promise you'll be safe", he kept staring at you and smiling, Wait here want to go check something", he said as he left. Ok sure, let me check out this place, There he was standing in front of me as I felt something pulling me to look at him. "We meet again, I'm Jimin Park by the way and I know who you are", he looked at me. Really? He came closer to me, inches from my lips as though he was about to kiss me. I have to admit I was aroused by the way he was looking at me and the way he kept licking his lower lip. I saw his fiery eyes as he got closer making my body just boil.

"Do I make you quiver? Are you scared?" He smirked. N-no, what makes you think that or even say that? "Look at the way you looking at me as though you want to devour me", he smirked. No way, I try and brush it off but his scent was just intoxicating, just great... "I'll see you around Luna", he left. I just froze there speechless. "You finished drooling over him hahahahahaha" Tae laughed at me. What? "I saw the way you looked at him but let me take you home", he smiled. Wait did you make us just meet on purpose? "I never said anything just a mere coincidence", he laughed again. Hmm really, thank you for taking me home bye...

I can't believe they would do that but why? Why were his stare and scent so intoxicating? I wanted to be around him, smell him, and just allow my body to take over this lust. "What's wrong Y/n, why are you looking so lost huh?" she asked. Don't want to talk about it... "Come on I saw Tae leaving you near home, are you seeing him now hmm?" she asked. Cut it out Lisa, need to get my thoughts in order aiiiishh. "Do any of those thoughts have to do with a guy named Jimin Park?" she looked me dead in the eyes but all I did is just freeze upon hearing his name, my fingers started shaking, who told you that? I asked her. My heart was racing so fast, if I were a car in a race I would be on my final lap right now, the shaking continued profusely. My body became weak to the question I was being asked but what puzzled me was the way my heart was beating.

Chapter 2

❝ Y/n what's wrong, you shaking, talk to me, please", she begged. It's nothing Lisa, let me rest. Are you still going to that party? "If you up for it yeah in a few hours." she looks at me. Need it dear need to clear my head? "We better rock it there will be hot guys there you know, and you need a man, a sexy man", she winks at you. Cut it out Lisa, I'm tired, please... "I know but you know I'm right", she winks again.

Why does his name make me utterly weak? Why am I so weak when I see or when I'm near him huh ?, Why do I want him so bad ?, I want to be close to him, and he makes me not stop thinking about him. Cut it out Y/n and focus on tonight at least he won't be there. I'll wear an LBD it always does the trick. "Woooow Y/n you look AMAZING and very hot", she looks at me from top to bottom. Thank you, you look beautiful too... "I'm only going for the boys and to get you a man hahaha", she winks at me. Do you ever get tired of troubling me huh? This girl please behave tonight and don't embarrass me. "I'll never get tired of loving you, let's go now we're already late", she drags me, and we make our way. We arrive at the place being ushered by two girls. "Welcome ladies, and enjoy yourselves", they smile at us. Thanks. "Yeah, yeah thanks, Y/n let me mingle, Will you be ok by yourself?" She looks at me. Yes, I'm going to get a drink and then hit the dance floor. People kept looking at me as if you were ravishing on the dance floor. "Hey beautiful, can I be your date tonight?" a strange man comes up to me. What the hell, leave me alone! "Why should I when you invite me in that sexy dress huh?" he looks at me licking his lips. Beat it and leave me ALONE, you evil peeve! The music gets louder. "I ain't leaving such a beauty alone", He grabs my hand pulling me away from the loud noise. Leave me alone, please!!!!!!...I keep fighting but he was too strong for me. Jimin and Taehyung come in looking hot and sexy. He stands in front of the guy. "Beat it or you'll regret it", he speaks with such authority. "Get lost, she is my date tonight hahaha", he pulls my hand. "Really??" he asks. He pushes the dude aside and pulls me by the waist placing a kiss on my lips. Leaving everyone shocked, I kiss him hungrily not refusing him. He pulls back. "Scram or you'll regret it", he looks at him with bloodshot eyes. "Sorry dude didn't know she was with you", he leaves. I look around for Lisa hoping she didn't witness that, shit, I just kissed Jimin and I liked it more than anything but, I don't care who saw that I've never wanted anyone like this. Jimin kept staring at me not moving. He pulls me closer to him not leaving any space between him and me. "You know you should stop looking this sexy, you'll make me lose my cool, and I love how you taste, I'll do it over and over again and you won't even refuse it", he smirked. I never said I'll accept it. "He kissed me passionately making the kiss last longer. I started breathing heavily while everyone kept watching the two of us but at that moment I didn't care. Then he stopped and pulled back. "No Luna not yet, you're not ready for me", he smirked. Why am I not fighting him? My body just worships him, I like how he smells and how he makes me feel. "Look at you, already blushing", he smirks. No, I'm not... "Shh Luna", he puts his finger on my lips, "don't deny it, I'll see you later", he leaves. "Hey Y/n, let's go before our reservation is canceled, Lisa called out to me". Okay, we leave and make it there, probably my lips were so swollen because of the way Jimin kissed me. "Now tell me what happened?" she asked. What do you mean? "How you locked lips with Jimin and you didn't tell me you knew him or what happened between you two", she looked at me. I don't know him, he just kissed me. "Come on Y/n what are you hiding from me", she asked. Drop it, can't you see how embarrassed I am now? I'm leaving now, I can't do this, I'll see you home, I stood and left, walking alone, I noticed it was a dark alley. I just wanted to get away from all this. I heard a noise and I got scared. "Shut up or we will kill you, but wait for you our dinner hahahahahaha", they laugh. "My breathing became heavy but I kept hiding. No matter what Y/n, don't move. "I check by the corner and notice 2 guys and one had blood on his mouth. "Where is that scent coming from? It's luring me to SWEETNESS", he started looking. "You can hide but I'll find you", they leave. What did I just witness, I fall to the ground, failing to keep straight. What did he mean he will find me? Will he kill me? I started crying, feeling scared. "Why are you crying, Luna?" Jimin asked looking at me. I hug him tightly. I'm scared, tears fall again. "Don't cry Luna, did he see you?" he looked at me. Who? "The guy you were hiding from?" he smirked. Wait how did you see that, were you following me? As you were speaking, he pushed me to the nearest wall kissing me. I want more but he's holding back, Jimin. "Shhhh, stop fighting it Luna, your scent is addictive, and your lips are so pleasant", he smirked. Thank you but can I go before they start looking for me? "Nah they not and I'm still busy with you", he smirks, "don't show me attitude or you'll get punished", he looked at me. Maybe it's what I want. "If you were ready you wouldn't be talking, you'll become a tigress I desire", he smirks grabbing me by the waist and making me bump into him. His muscles are so strong, and him showing his dominant side was very hot, I want you now Jimin. "My Luna is hungry, he smirks. He kisses me passionately like a lion attacking its prey. Truthfully I was. He held me gently but the desire made me kiss him passionately again not stopping. I needed him but he wasn't letting go. Something stopped him.

Chapter 3

❝ I'm going, for now, Will find you don't worry", he smiles at me. Don't go, please. "Don't worry you'll be safe. Tae will take you home", he kissed me, leaving me breathless and hot for his touch. "Hey heard I'm the one taking you home", Tae smiles. Wait, did you just see all that? "You'll get your answers soon, don't worry", he smiles again. Why did that guy have blood on his mouth? "Don't worry about Y/n, please", he looked at me with begging eyes. If you not answering me, I will go home by myself, I want to know, who are you? "You won't drop this will you?" he looked at me. No, tell me. "Jimin will tell you when he's ready", he looked at me. No, he won't tell me, NOW! Tae, please. "No Y/n, I've said enough, Jimin will give you answers, let's go, I get you home safely hmmm", he smiled at me. Ok, I'm sorry, I just want answers, and I'm confused. "I know all in good time my dear, here we are, and I will see you around Y/n", he smiled again. Okay, thanks Tae. "Y/n, I'm so sorry, I didn't mean to, I was really worried about you, I'm sorry", Lisa looked at me. It's ok, the walk did me good, I feel better now, talk in the morning, and love you. "Ok, goodnight", I left. What did I witness last night? What are they hiding? Why do I feel they have known me for a long time? Why am I not getting answers? Tonight, I'm seeing Jimin and I need an answer, he will be ready to answer me because I'm ready for him. Y/n, what are you doing? You barely know him and yet you want him so bad, why am I so drawn to him, I want him to touch me, damn these confusing hormones and feelings. "Y/n come down, you have to see this" she calls me. Ok, coming. I make my way there.

"Morning, how are you today? You look tired", uncle Kai greeted me. Morning, yes uncle, I haven't rested from the time we came, how are you? "I'm ok saddened by this", he shows me a picture, and a letter which read ***"This is just the beginning, you'll know who we are"***, and the picture showed a man who was tortured and bruised and then killed. Who could do such a horrible thing uncle? "I don't know, but we will find them, I want you girls safe, make sure you are always with someone when going somewhere", he pleads with me. "Oh don't worry uncle, especially about Y/n hahaha", she laughs at the way I was feeling so shy. Don't start Lisa, Uncle I'm going over for a sleepover at my friend's place, is it ok? "It's ok, just make sure you are safe always, call me if you need me", he hugs me as I leave.

Jimin P.o.v

What have you done JK, if they find out, you will expose us. "I don't care, I did what I did because I wanted to, and I will do more hahaha", Jungkook laughed. Stop being foolish, I punch him. "Try and stop me, your pretty girl will be mine, even though you hide her from me Jiminahhh I will find her, I'll endeavor her slowly in front of you hahaha", he laughs. "Cut it out you two, Jungkook just STOP!!!" Tae pleaded. "Why so you two can rule, might I remind you, I'm the alpha now, I'm your alpha now, respect that NOW, or I'll kick you out", he looked at me. You know you can't, you need me for protection and you know I'm stronger than you. "We will see Jimin and Tae might I remind you a half breed, if it goes out, they will kill you, half vampire, half-wolf hahaha, and we brothers, what are the odds hahaha", he laughed. "Stop it Jungkook, before you lose your alpha title right now", he punches him. "Yes, bring it", he spits out blood, "I'm leaving for now hahaha", he laughed. I won't be around, going somewhere. "You seeing her aren't you?" he looks at me. I believe she wants answers, I will give her them before Jk ruins everything. "Be honest, she's a good girl, don't blow it ok", he looks at me. What makes you think I will? "I know you Jimin, remember", he looks at me. I've fallen deep for her, what if she rejects me or thinks I'm a freak? If she rejects me will I have to kill her to protect her from Jk? "No, she won't reject you, I'm there", he smirks. Thanks for always having my back, I'll see you later. "Kul, always, that's what brothers are for", I leave.

Y/n P.o.v

Where will I find him? I need to see him now! Where are you Jimin? We need to talk, I n- need answers, Let me check where we once met I might find him there. I find him sitting, waiting for me, I make my way to him. Hey. "Hey Luna, I knew you were looking for me", he grabs me making you sit on his lap. How do you know that huh? "Cause I can read that beautiful mind of yours", he winks at me. Is it? "You want answers, I'm giving them to you slowly, he bites my ear lobe, I know just how much you want me, desire me, you think I'm holding back", he looks at me. Ohh really and what do I want now huh? "Come I show you then", he takes my hand and leads me somewhere. "Are you hungry Luna?" he asks. I am but my food is refusing to come to me. "My Luna is in a hurry", he smirks. You smell good, I shoved my hands in his hair and kissed him while sucking his tongue, noticing how much he liked it, his hands were sliding over my back, making me moan a little. "Luna, you like that don't you?" I wrap my hands around his shoulders deepening the kiss.

Y/n P.o.v

I kissed his mouth like a hungry cub getting ready to eat, nibbling on his lower lip, and stroking my tongue along his, he grabbed my waist, his chest heaving. "What are you doing to me Y/n, I don't want to hurt you", he smirked. I ran my hands down his chest, feeling the hardness of his muscle. I want you Jimin, I need you, you driving me crazy right now. He grabbed my thighs, his hands beneath the edge of my dress. "You so wet and I barely touched you", he smirks, "I'll try not to hurt you", he looked into my eyes. Just do it Jimin, I NEED THIS!

He pushed his thumb inside me, biting his lower lips as I gripped onto his. The scent of our lust was heavy and humid in the air, a seductive mix of need and pheromones that awakened every cell in my body, I felt like something was taking over me, unzipping his pants, I felt like I possessed him, I closed my eyes. "You so tight, I'll be gentle, I promise Luna", he smirked. You so big, tears fell as he entered me, J—Jimin it hurts......... be gentle. "I can't stop, fuck you feel so good", he captured me by the neck as the orgasm exploded through us, starting with the ecstatic spasms of mine and his radiating outward beastlike roar until I trembled, I moaned and came harder my body jerking with every pulse of pleasure, he was still inside me, I could feel his member still in me, he never took his eyes off me. "Fuck, fuck, fuck", pounding his hips up at me, "Luna, you driving me crazy", he came with an animal sound of feral ecstasy, a snarling release that riveted me with its ferocity, he shook as the orgasm tore into him. I couldn't take it again, he made me cum for him again. "Luna come here", resting my face on his chest as we control our breathing. "I'm sorry I hurt you", he looked at me. I'm ok Jimin, are you ok? "I gotta go, I'm fine", he kissed me. Wait, why are you leaving, did I do anything? As I noticed blood on my legs, did he just use me to get what he wanted? Why did I agree to this if I had known, tears fell, men are all just the same. I tried to stand but I collapsed and fainted losing a lot of blood..

Chapter 4

H-help me please, I collapse again losing a lot of blood. "What happened to her doctor???" Lisa asked. "She has lost a lot of blood, please may I speak to you, young lady?" Doctor Jin requested. "Yes doctor, what's the matter?" she asked. "Was she raped or had any sexual activities?" Doctor Jin asked. "As far as I know, she is a virgin or was a virgin, why?" she asked. "It does seem like she was raped, she lost so much blood....She has a lot of scars which are worrisome to me", the doctor looked at his chat. "Will she wake up or what doc?" she asked looking worried. I cough, w-where am I? Answer me, anyone? Tears fell. "Hey, hey, you at the hospital", Lisa replied. What happened, why am I in so much pain? "Calm down Y/n, you need to rest, you lost a lot of blood, and can you tell us what happened?" he asked. I don't want to talk about it. Tears fell again. "Were you raped? Tell me you'll be safe Y/n", uncle Kai asked. I wasn't rapped, please may I not talk about it, PLEASE? "Ok Y/n, be safe always and I hope you get better soon", he looked at me. Can I and Lisa get some privacy, also thank you for being here uncle, means everything to me. "Ok my dear, see you later, let me get back to work", he smiled. Thank you uncle for everything, I love you and be safe too. "You're welcome, I'll see you girls", he leaves.

Jimin P.o.v

What did I do? I have to stay away from her, so much blood, her scent is too strong, I just had to leave, and I couldn't control myself, blood, her blood. Her blood is so strong. "Jimin, calm down, I've never seen you like this", Tae rushed to my side. Leave me Tae, I need blood before I rip out something. "Calm down first, Grab the blood we keep for times like this", he gives me and I drink the blood. Thanks, Tae, I've messed up big time, I hurt Y/n. "How bad is it? Tae looks at me. She's in hospital and she had passed out. "Whaaaaaattt? Did you tell her what you are, what we are?" he looks at me. No, we got lost in the moment, I was afraid of losing her Tae, she'll never want a monster like me, I'm leaving her, and I want her safe not dead. "Naah man, you know she's your mate, we both saw it, and she'll forgive you don't worry, she is a good person", he slaps me. I'll stay away from her to keep her safe, I can be able to keep her alive. "You not thinking straight, go rest will talk later, will go check on her", He smiles at me. Thank you for everything.

Y/n P.o.v

"What happened Y/n? Talk to me please", she sits next to me, brushing my face. I slept with him and he left me just like that. "Y/n what? I'll kill him when I see him", she looks angrily at me. Leave him, I'm tired really, I Th......ought he was.......I started crying uncontrollably. "Ok when you ready dear we will deal with him, see you later", she leaves. Ok thanks, dear, I love you, bye. "Hie, Can I come in?" Tae looks at me. What do you want, did he send you huh? "Nah I came to tell you what he failed to tell you", he sits next to me. Ok come, I'm listening. "Jimin, myself, and Jungkook are different", he looks at me. Different yes, but why is that important? "Jimin and Jungkook are vampires, I, on the other hand, am a half-breed", he looks at me like he was waiting for a response. Half-breed how? "Half-human, half-vampire, and why are you not freaking out?" he looks at me. I knew already, just wanted to see if Jimin had the guts to tell me, "Will you want to see him again? He looks at me. Yes, he owes me that much, if he doesn't then I'm done. "Ok Y/n be strong isn't", he smiles at me. Thanks, Tae, see you around

Y/n P.o.v

I finally get to go out today, I appreciate Lisa for suggesting we go shopping especially dresses, I'm now better starting a new job and school although, I miss him, I miss his touch, I miss his....I start crying. "Knock, knock why are you crying Y/n hmmm?" she looks at me. I miss him, Lisa, I know it mustn't be like this. "It's ok let's go shopping, I know you'll feel better when we come", she smiles at me. Ok, give me a few minutes will be ready. "Yeah that's my Y/n, hurry, hurry", she laughs. I make my way downstairs, feeling heroic in every movement as I rocked those heels. We got to the mall and entered a boutique. Wow all these dresses Lisa, will I try them all? "Please feel free, enjoy yourselves girls", the worker welcomes us. "Thank you, we will be long, need to get this girl in sexy clothes", she smirks. Lisa you gotta stop trying to get me a date I can do it by myself. Ohh are you saying you're back in the market?" she smirks. I'm saying I'm now busy loving myself, will get myself a date when I'm ready. "Yeah girl, I'm proud of you, she hugs me, now get in there and try some dresses will see you when you are done. As I was dressing I felt hands grab my waist tight. What the h-hell. As I noticed Jimin turning me to face him. "HI Y/n, I miss your sweet scent", he kissed my neck. J-Jimin, my body couldn't resist him. Why are you here? You left me, remember that part?, as I was speaking he kissed me. Jimin what are you doing? "What I was supposed to do that day, I'm sorry Y/n for leaving you that day, I didn't want to hurt you, you are very special to me my Luna, I never want to hurt you, your blood is like a drug to me, I get so weak when I am near you", he looks into my eyes. I'm sorry, I know it was hard for you too but I was very hurt, you just left me. Just keep this in mind: "YOU ARE MINE Y/N, he kissed me again, I'll see you around and by the way, this dress looks very sexy on you", he smirks. Hmmm, I like it too, Lisa will like it too. "My Luna, I'm leaving now, we'll pick this up soon", he kisses me. Lisa, what do you think? "Woooow you look hot in that dress, I LOVE IT, let's go grab something to eat and we rock our new style hahaha, she laughs. Good idea, I'm so hungry, she notices something about me. "Where did you get that mark Y/n the one on your neck?" she observes it. What mark? I check myself and notice a black mark behind my ear as though it was a bite, I hurt myself while bathing, I'm sorry Lisa can't tell you this but Jimin will have to tell me what he did. "Hmmm ok, let's get out here", we pay for our stuff and make our way. Thank you Lisa for doing this with me. "You shouldn't thank me that is what family is for, you are my best friend Y/n and I wouldn't trade you for anything", she hugs me. You to Lisa got mad love for you. As I look up notice someone coming up to us. "Hello beautiful ladies", he greeted us but knowing who he was I became very scared. H—hello, I smiled. "You look ravishingly hot", he smirked. "I just couldn't stay away I was drawn to you", he smirks again. I noticed Lisa looking at me winking her eye and licking her lips in mockery of me, he noticed the mark on your neck and he smirked. Thank you...Please excuse me I need to go to the ladies. "Take all the time in the world, I know that beauty didn't come cheap", he winks at me. What is he doing here? My heart can't stop pounding fast, what does he want huh? Tae told me he the alpha and he was a killer, I felt someone grab my hand. "Let's get out here, you're not safe, I'll explain to you, Tae will take Lisa home", Jimin takes my hand. Ok, I trust you, He holds my hand tightly not letting go, Jimin I'm tired, and I can't go further. "Ok Luna, let's rest here, we will be safe", he makes me sit. Thank you for everything. "I'm sorry for putting your life in danger Luna, stay here I want to check out the area", he kisses me. Wait before you go, why did you mark me? "BECAUSE YOU ARE MINE, JUST MINE, and I will do everything to protect you my sweet Luna", he smiled at me. Jimin, I kissed him. "We start this I won't stop and I'll hurt you", he smirked. I know but I trust you Jimin. "Stay here will be back", he leaves. I hear strange sounds escalating. What to do? Jimin has been gone for a long time. "You thought you could run away from me Y/n?" he laughs. Please leave me alone I don't want any problems. "We will see about that just calm down and don't worry Jimin is not coming to your aid this time", he laughed as I felt a stinging pain on my arm as I passed out onto his arms. W—where am I? Someone help me. I noticed my feet chained together. My dress was torn apart scars all over my body, fear overtook me. "WELCOME TO YOUR NEW HOME", Jungkook laughed.

Chapter 5

Why are you doing this? Please let me go, I didn't do anything I started hitting the door with your weak palms, Please, my voice became faint. "Shut it or you'll not leave, hahaha you not leaving you my food now", He appears in front of me, his eyes dark and bloody like a hunter marking its prey. "Y/n stop fighting, you just a weak thing, I'll devour you slowly and leave the bones for Jimin hahahahahaha", he laughed. I spit at him. Leave me alone, I hate you an evil monster and I'm not afraid of you. "Ohh really?" he comes close at a fast speed pulling your hair hard and hurting you till drops of blood are seen. He tastes my blood. "Ohh Y/n you shouldn't have done that, he pulled my neck close to him, but not yet hahaha", he pushes me to the floor hurting my knee. Ouch my knee, I'll get out of here. "I want to see you try Y/n, I want to see how far you'll go" he smirks locking the door as he leaves.

Jimin P.o.v

Where are you Jungkook, Using the Chinese herbs to hide hmm? "Jimin leave now or I'll kill you here as the alpha's orders", Jin appears. No, I'm not leaving here, tell that crony Jungkook, I'm not afraid. "Choose your words wisely boy", Jin looks at me. Or what? Suddenly two guys appear and shoot a pin on your shoulder as you pass out. Where am I, I notice Tae sitting next to me. Tae, wake up, wake up. "What happened, I came towards you and everything went black. We were tranquilized by vampire blood which if we drank we die, Jk will pay for this. I'm done with him he has crossed all lines. Where is Y/n, is she safe, I can't find her scent anywhere. "Let's first focus on getting out of her then we find her", he looked at me. You're right, one thing Jungkook forgets is that I am the strongest Vamp in the clan, he thought he could beat this, I pull breaking the door and opening it, six vampires come attacking us, and I break their bones as you leave Tae lights them on fire.

Y/n P.o.v

Why is this happening to me, I have to get out of here, Y/n come on you can do it, prove to him you are not weak, he might have tasted my blood but he didn't kill me by mistake, as I pick a nail and by coincidence, the chains come out. Yes, yes, I did it now with this window am sure I can free myself and run no stopping Y/n once we are out, I push the window opening cutting myself and I run not looking back, till I hit a log and fell hurting my ankle. I-I have to continue, I stand as I limp and running not seeing where I was going as tears clouded my eyes, I trip and fall, and all becomes blurry.

Jimin P.o.v

I can smell her, I'm close to her, and I see her falling in the water my heart beat fast as I ran faster than lightening catching her as we were dragged in the water by heavy and painful currents, I pulled her close to me, kissing her giving her breath, Y/n please be ok, I pulled her out and administer mouth to mouth.

Y/n P.o.v

I let out a cough, Jimin, I hug him not letting go. Thank you. Tae appears. "Sorry guys but Jimin need your strength, I'll take Y/n to a safe place", he looks at me. "Luna will you be ok?" he asks. Go, I'm in safe hands, I kiss him bye. We arrived at a safe house, it looked cozy and warm. "You need anything Y/n? Come let me clean these cuts", he sits me down. Thanks, how come my blood doesn't affect you? "I'm also human Y/n, I eat food too so your scent isn't strong for me", he smiles. Ohh I see, it starts getting cold, and I started shaking.

Tae P.o.v

Gosh, she looked so beautiful when she was smiling, why am I falling for her so much, I want to have her, be her man, fuck this is so wrong. Tae, I shiver profusely, please keep me warm.

Y/n P.o.v

I just wanted warmth, I don't care what happens to me as I felt his warm hands come around me, and he smelt good. "Better?' he looked at me. Yes. He suddenly cupped my cheeks, kissing me, my body froze against him as I felt his warm lips on mine, I deepened the kiss as though I had never kissed before I couldn't stop myself, and he let go. "Fuck, I'm s-sorry Y/n", we were disturbed by a knock. Please don't go. "I gotta check who it is, no one knows this place except me and Jimin. "Hello Kim Taehyung", Suga stood there, the last of the vampire doctors.

Chapter 6

"What are you doing here?" Tae asked the strange vampire. "Jimin sent me, I gotta check up on her, she lost a lot of blood", he said. "As you can see she's ok, let her sleep, she's been through a lot", Tae frowned. "Cool, I shall return later then", he looks at Tae and leaves.

Y/n P.o.v

I woke up with puffy eyes, sneezing a lot as I notice Tae's hands still around me. Tae, I sneeze, you'll get sick if you stay next to me, wake up, he wakes up looking puzzled and worried, how could someone be so sexy upon waking up, what's going on with me? "Suga is coming he will give you meds, he feels my head, you're burning up, let's go I give you a warm bath", he smiles at me. Ok but you'll have to be patient I can't walk properly, as I was talking, he carried me, Tae what are you doing? "You need a bath Y/n, don't fight it", he looked at me.

Jimin P.o.v

Jungkook you shouldn't have done that, now you will lose your alpha title, I challenge you to be alpha. "What the hell, no", he looks at me. It's in our laws and you can't change that. "I can if I want to", he smirks. I'll see you in a few weeks, May the strongest win I smirked, probably that will be me. "We will see, he looked angrily as I left.

Y/n P.o.v

Why is my body so weak against them? "You want me to leave? He looks at me. No, bath me, please. "Are you sure Y/n?" he looks at me. I didn't ask you, bathe me. "Ok", he removed my bathrobe and started bathing me, he pushed me close to him and kissed me passionately allowing no room for me to breathe, as my whole body touched him. Desire. Passion. Lust or was it my hormones talking?

Tae P.o.v

Damn she tastes so sweet, Jimin will kill me if he finds out, I find the will to stop, sorry Y/n, I can't do this. He leaves not looking back.

Y/n P.o.v

What the hell, I guess he did not like it, is there anything wrong I did, I limp out of the room and wear a red dress, I'm so hungry aaaiiissshhh let me go see if there is food. As I made the food I felt his warm hands around my waist. "I'm sorry Y/n, I didn't mean to leave you, and I couldn't hurt you", he looks at me. It's ok, I hu....*he kisses me and I deepen the kiss but I stopped, No Tae, please stop. "What's wrong?" he looks at me worried. I feel tired, he ran his finger on my swollen lips. "I'm so hungry for you and I will have you". He smirks as he leaves. I wake up and find Jimin sitting next to me, watching me sleep as thick brown-red blood dripped from his head. "I'm sorry Y/n, please heal me, and clean me", he said. When did you come? "Just now and all I could think of is you, Luna, heal me.

Chapter 7

Y/n P.o.v

Jimin, what happened, why are you bleeding heavily? As I spoke he passed out on my weak arms. Jimin, wake up, tears fell, Jimin wake up please, please wake up, I panicked and put him comfortably while cleaning his blood, he looked so much in pain. Why is he in so much pain, what happened? He woke up ferociously attacking me but he was able to control himself calming down. "Get away from me Y/n, I don't want to hurt you", he looked down. I can help, I can give you my blood, p—please let me help you. "What if I can't stop Luna", he looks at me. You'll find the will to stop, I trust you Jimin. He kissed me while tears emitted from his eyelids as he bit into my neck, he looked like he wasn't going to stop, my blood tasted so sweet and was like a painkiller to him, he couldn't stop, he was almost killing me, but he stopped when he noticed I was passing out, he paused and everything went black.

Jimin P.o.v

I told you, Luna, Once I started I wasn't going to stop, is it because I'm in love with you ?, what is this strange feeling I have succumbed to it makes me want to abdicate to your beautiful being, I want you Luna, to continue what we started. As I lay down in her arms I kissed her while tears fell.

Y/n P.o.v

Jimin, I Coughed, why are you crying? I spoke with a faintly weak voice. "I'm sorry Luna, I almost killed you", he looked at me. But you didn't which is good isn't it Jimin, no words came out. Why are you so frigid Jimin, come I warm you up. "You almost died and yet you can still make me want you like right now", he smirked. Is it wrong that I'm lusting for those dark and dangerous eyes looking at me? How my body craved those lips, I admit I was weak for Jimin my body worshipped him, he dominated every lustful pulse of pleasure I wanted. "Luna what you thinking?" he looked at me. Nothing I smiled at him knowing the dark thoughts I was having, can you help me unzip my dress, please? "Hmm ok", he came close, his breath on me giving me Goosebumps as he unzips me, I turned around and placed a kiss on his lips. "Y/n, you bad girl made me fall for that", he smirked. Stop talking and let your lips talk, touching mine, I kissed him, this time deepening the kiss, he bites my neck leaving hickeys, and he touched my swollen lips with his finger. "Don't start something you won't finish", he looked at me. Who told you I won't finish it as you went closer hugging him not letting go.

Jimin P.o.v

Fuck she's so beautiful, what if I hurt her like last time? How do I tell her I love her? "Jimin, are you ok, want to tell me what happened, who hurt you?" she asked. Let me tell you, Luna.

Time Skipped to time I was hurt

So you think you can come at me and win Jin, you're a doctor vampire you should know better, just because Jungkook is afraid to lose huh?, no wonder Suga is the best of his kind unlike you, a wanna-be. "You shouldn't have challenged him", he looks at me. I'm not afraid of him, he will see my wrath, I've tolerated him for hundreds of years now it's time he sees what I am capable of. "Don't be foolish Jimin", he looks at me again. Or what? Two vampires came at me with full force attacking me, I dodged their attack, hitting them suddenly one hits me on the head while the other one stabbed me. You'll pay for that, I pulled them together killing them brutally, merciless. I have to find Y/n, she's the only one who can heal me, the one I need, and she's my soulmate, my life.

Time skipped back

Who could have done such a nefarious thing to you, why are they trying to kill you? "Because I challenged Jungkook to be alpha, if I lose they break my bones and burn them so it's a risk I'll take to protect you", he looked at me. "I Lo..." the doorbell rang. Don't go Jimin, please I'm scared. "I have to check who it is, Tae is covering for me, so he and I only know this place", he looks at me. Ok, be safe.

Jimin P.o.v

What the hell do you want Suga, didn't you say you never going to show up? "Like I told Tae you both are playing a dangerous game, trust me, I'm here to check on her, remember she lost a lot of blood", he smirked. Do it and leave Suga, I don't want to see you near her EVER. "Whatever, like I want to be here", he goes to Y/n's room.

Y/n P.o.v

Is he ok? Who was that, I hear a knock, come in. "Hi I'm Suga, I'm sure Tae told you I was coming", he looked at me. Yes he did, is anything wrong? He examined me, and he finally finished. "I'll see you in a week with the results", he smiled. "What's wrong with her?" Jimin asked. "I'll let you know when it's the full moon, by the way, did you intake her blood?" he looks at Jimin. Yes and I've never felt such strength, I want her blood", He replied. "Let's wait till the full moon we see the effects" Suga insists. "Cool, go now Suga, and better make sure no one sees you", Jimin gives him a stern look. "Hahaha we will see", he leaves. Jimin are you ok I noticed him sitting down, deep in thought.

"Yeah, I'm ok", He pulled me making me sit on his lap, I held onto him, heads touching each other. I'm Ravenous for you Jimin, I'm afraid of what I'll do if I don't have you now. "I won't do anything to hurt you", he smirked. I ferociously kiss him, biting him, he lets out a moan as I noticed how much he liked it, and you make me crazy for you. I kissed him deep till he sobbed, ripping the comforter in his fists, the tearing sound reverberating through the enclosed space, turned me on even more. "Luna, I want to be inside you NOW as he clinched tight on my breast kissing me on the neck, he pushed his finger inside making me moan a little, Luna if you feel pain let me know I don't want to hurt you", he smirked. I know Jimin, as I swayed my hips on top of him. Shh I've got you", As I climaxed in a search of pleasure, his growl was a sound of pure animal sexuality, that was so hot damn, he made me lie flat as he removed all clothing I had on. "fuck you so beautiful Luna", As he kissed my breasts liking the moan I let out, he kissed me on my bellybutton leaving marks, as he opened my legs slowly kissing my thighs. Jimin hmmm, don't stop, please. He smirked, " you like that don't you?", as he played with his fingers near my cunt while he kissed me, "you so wet Y/n, fuck", as he unzipped his shorts letting out a soft warm moan, he pushed deep inside me. Ji......min, I cried in pleasure. "Hush you so tight Luna", he smirked. Mm, he made me climax again as his member swelled up in response to the covetous milking of my body, I liked that a lot. He watched me fall apart with those haunting dark eyes, his control absolute, he didn't move, just held himself deep enhancing the connection between us, I just kissed him as I pressed my fingers into his hair. His teeth caught my lower lip, sinking gently into the swollen curve, he thrusted faster making animal sexual sounds. He was a beast. My beast. "Luna, fuck, fuck, I'm cumin, I felt him spurting inside me, filling me as I trembled with another orgasm, the pleasure pulsing gently through me, I lay my cheek on his chest, listening to his pounding heart, his perspiration mingling with me, I calmed down. You won't leave me like last time? "No Luna, you precious to me, he kept on looking at me as I lay on top and close to him, I hurt you, Luna, I'm sorry, I didn't mean to"., he looked at me. I'm ok Jimin, I fall asleep, and a loud text awakens me, who the hell is texting this late? "You'll never know till you check Luna", he smiled.

TEXT READ: Hie its Rose, I'm with uncle and Lisa now, come home Y/n NOW !!!!!!!!!!!!!

Chapter 8

Y/n P.o.v

Jimin I have to go. "Why, what's wrong?" he looks at me. My sister is waiting for me she sounds worried, she never calls or texts me. "You want us to go together", he winks at me. No way, are you crazy, my uncle would kill you, especially since I didn't tell him about you yet. "Ok Y/n, I'll see you but I'll leave you home", he kissed me. Thanks for understanding I kissed him again. Hi Rose, She slapped me. What ...Tears fell. "How dare you do that huh? Mom called you and you never responded, do you know how worried she is, she's at the hospital, it's bad we going now", she said angrily. No Rose, I can't just leave now please understand. "I'll give you a day to pack but we are leaving", she said. Tears fell, now I had to leave Jimin, he won't take it lightly, I can't separate from him, he's my drug as I am his and I will tell him how I feel tonight, I called him, it rang once and he answered. "Hello Luna", he smiled. Hi J—Jimin. "Are you ok? You sound sad", he asked. Let's meet at a restaurant we need to talk. "Ok, the one you like right?" he laughs. Geez yes, it's ok, that one. I cut the call and get ready. As I go, I heard someone call me. "Y/n, Y/n wait up", she calls out to me. "Keren Lee my gosh it's been so long, I screamed seeing my long-lost friend, happiness just overshadowed me. I'm so happy to see you, it's been years we should meet for drinks and catch up. "Yes please, I missed you and I have so much to tell you", she smiled. "Ok let me save your number", she hugs me again before she leaves, wow she's looking good.

Jimin P.o.v

I know she's leaving but I have to tell her how I feel before I lose her, I feel she deserves to know the truth. She arrives in front of me, so beautiful, I lose words every time she's with me, and she's a goddess in my eyes. Hie", she smiled.

Y/n P.o.v

My palms are sweating, profusely, I'm so nervous, will he receive my love? "You look breathtakingly hot and beautiful", he kisses me. Thank you, I took a seat. "Are you ok? You didn't sound ok", he looked at me. I'm ok but I have something to tell you, I'm leaving for home but will come back when my mother is better. "I can't leave you", he looked at me. I know listen, I love you and I've wanted to tell you that the first day we shared our first kiss. "Why would you love a monster like me?" He leaves and absconds. How could he leave just like that? Doesn't he feel the same about me? After all, we have been through? As I was about to leave someone grabbed my hand. "Where you think you going?" Jungkook looked at me. Please leave me alone, my heart started beating fast. "Not this time, you see you my prey, how can I let you go?" He grabs me by the waist pulling me close to him. His hold was very strong. "You ran away from me, now you'll watch what I do, I want you ready for a ball later tonight", he smirked. No, please. "You want me to kill you or kill that sweet sister of yours huh?" he smirked again. Tears fell. No please stop, I'll be ready. "Good girl, I'll come to pick you up", he smirked.

Jimin P.o.v

I couldn't tell her, why? I just ran, what a coward, I've waited for this girl my life hundreds of years my heart beats for her, that's the only thing I have, I can't lose it. "Yoh Jimin, why are you so lost in thought?" Tae sits next to me. "It's about Y/n isn't it?" he asked. Maybe, I'm fighting Jungkook tonight after the ball, if anything happens take care of Y/n and tell her I love her. "Nah you'll tell her yourself", he looked at me seriously. I don't want to see her Tae, she won't like a monster like me. "Jimin, calm down will you, she already does", he said. Stop acting as if you care, I know you kissed her. "And I wanted to and I never hid that from you", he still looked at me. Do you think she'll like you after she finds out what you did to her sister Rose huh? "Don't bring her up", he punched me. Or what? Hahaha, you think you can hide it forever? "I'll die trying, even if it means I take you out", he punched me hard as blood started dripping from my nose. I'm going, to take care of her.

Y/n P.o.v

Omg, what do I do about this? My life is a mess, first Jimin, now this, I have to protect the family. "Hey, girl where you lost?" Lisa asked. Huh, I'm not, just thinking. "I'm worried about you", she looked at me. I'm fine Lisa, help me get ready. "Where are you going, don't you have to pack?" she asked again. Don't ask questions, just help me get ready. Ok don't eat me, was just worried", she smiles. Whatever I finally get ready wearing a cute white dress. "Where are you going dressed like this Y/n?" Rose studied me from top to bottom. Saying bye to friends, it's not like you care anyway. "Stop lying", I kept walking as she talked not wanting her to know the truth. Jungkook arrives wearing a suit and looking irresistibly handsome. "You look beautiful Y/n, you better drop this attitude right now", he looks at me as he grabs me by the chin. Thank you, I faintly smiled, he pulled me by the waist and kept me there all the time, close to him, I got it Jungkook, please don't hurt my family. "Nah I'm not promising you that hahaha we will see how you do tonight", he smirked. We arrived at the place, it was mixed with humans and vampires, a small vampire boy welcomed us. "Welcome my alpha and guest, you must be Y/n?" he said. Yes, thank you. "I've heard so much about you from Jimin", he smiled. "Ohh he", I shut him up, I'm sorry I'm with Jungkook tonight, please remember who your alpha is. They all bow to Jungkook, except Jimin and Tae. Oh my manners, please proceed, enjoy yourselves". He smiled. Thank you I smiled back at him. "Doing very well Y/n, I see how that pathetic life of yours is so precious to you hahahahahaha", he smirked. Just keep your end of the deal. "I plan to dearest Y/n", he smells my scent, and we sit at a high table as though you were a married couple. "I WILL NEVER BOW TO YOU JUNGKOOK, even if I took my last breath", Jimin looked Jungkook dead in the eyes. "We will see, He hadn't noticed me as his eyes were deep red, time to do the couple dance, leave all that for later", Jungkook smirked again. Does he know how handsome he is when he looks angry, Y/n why do you care for him, he doesn't care about you. "Are you ready for our dance? Remember Y/n any funny business Rose dies, am I clear?" he looked at me. Yes Jungkook, I've heard you loud and crystal clear. He stood taking my hand as the music slowly started grabbing my waist pushing me close to his chest, he hardened his grip hurting me a little. You are hurting me, I'm doing everything you are saying, so keep your word, and stop hurting me. "Hahahaha I do what I want, I'll be back, mingle with others, don't try anything, my boys are watching you", he smirks. I know, he leaves. Finally, I can breathe. "Make sure the incense is ready that Jimin mustn't win at all cost am I clear?" Jungkook plotted. "Yes my Alpha, a mysterious vampire responded. This place is so boring, I made my way to the top of the stairs, it was quieter but nice, and I felt cold as I felt someone grabbing me by the waist and gently kissing my neck. Jimin as I turned around and hugged him, I hate you, you always leave me, why? He kissed me. "I love you, Luna, I'm sorry I left, I was afraid of hurting you", he smiled. Stop being afraid Jimin, you are strong enough to beat Jungkook, then be alpha, don't die on me, I love you. I kiss him as he lets go, and one of Jungkook crooks comes grabbing you. "Don't even think of it", Jimin started getting angry. "Just following orders, the miss, is wanted or a Rose will be hurt", he laughed. Jimin it's okay, remember to beat him no matter what. "Ok Luna, I'll be seeing you around". He winked at me. "Where had you gone huh?" he angrily grabs me. Just a quiet place wanted to be by myself. "You better not be lying to me Y/n", he looks at me. I'm not, Knowing Jimin was watching he grabbed my hair pulling me close to him, he kissed me biting my lips. Tears fall, leave me alone, I noticed Jimin getting angry his eyes had changed color.

Chapter 9

Jimin stop please, I'm sorry, I stood in front of Jungkook. "Get away from him NOW!!!" Jimin shouted. No Jimin, you won't hurt him, I'm not moving, and he pushed me hurting me. Tears fell. Jimin, I love you. "Stop it Y/n", he angrily shouted. I love you. "I'm sorry Y/n, are you ok?" Jungkook helped me up. Yes, I'm fine, thank you as I stood next to him. "I'll be seeing you later Jimin", Jungkook smirked.

Jimin P.o.v

Jungkook, You pushing it, this won't weaken me, I'll do all I can to be alpha, I know you'll cheat, but I'll be ready. "Yoh Jimin are you ready?" one of Jung kook's crooks asked. Yes, why are you here?" from nowhere he attacked me. Ohh he's trying to weaken me, he will not succeed, and they beat me up so badly weakening me.

Y/n P.o.v

Where is Jimin, as you here sounds, Jimin, no stop it, you are killing him? "Stay out of this miss Y/n, we were told not to hurt you but if you disturb us we will hurt you", they looked at me. Stop it, I pushed them and one hit me making me fall and hurt myself. "Y/n, are you ok?" He pushed up attacking them and killing them. Jimin, are you ok? You bleeding. Jungkook is cheating, I don't want him to win over me", he looked at me. You won't, I have something to tell you but first take my blood Jimin, don't argue or refuse, and you'll be stronger. "I can't", he looked at me. Just do it, please. Ok, He kissed me first, then bit me till

I passed out. "Tae, take Y/n out of here and make sure she's safe", Jimin instructed Tae. "Yes, be safe", Tae responded as Jimin's eyes turned blue.

Jimin P.o.v

This power is different, what is happening to me? I arrive at Jung kook's place. Jungkook, let's start this you thought you would cheat huh? "No how is that possible you're supposed to be weak, why are you so strong he attacked me making me squeal, hahaha you'll never beat me, even if you try", as he poured Chinese herbs mixed with Thai but misses. Nah, not today Jungkook, I'll be back but now acknowledge me as alpha, or I will kill you. "Never", he attacks me again but misses. Do it now. "I acknowledge you as my alpha we are not done yet", he frowned. Yes, we are by law, if you go beyond me you'll be killed by a human. "I know", he frowned again.

Y/n P.o.v

Tae where is Jimin? I screamed and tried to stand but my legs refused for me to stand. "Take it easy Y/n, you just lost some blood", Tae pleaded with me. I don't care, I want to be with Jimin, NOW!!!! . "No Y/n, you can't see him like that", he pleaded again. I have to tell him what Suga told me everything. "What did he tell you?" he looked at me.

Recap to Suga dialogue

"Y/n what I tell you, don't tell anyone, especially Jimin", Suga spoke. What is wrong with me? "You are the descendent of our guardian vampire and your blood carries healing power", he smiled. What are you talking about, not possible, how could that be true? "It is your great-grandmother, who had a lover who was the guardian of all vampires", he spoke. How come my mother never told me? "That she will tell you herself, did you not notice how strong Jimin became after he took your blood, his blood became mixed with yours, you are one with him, he's now your soulmate, and you are supposed to tell him you are pregnant", he shocked me with that last statement. What, no I'm not, how is that possible with a vampire, it's rare. "You have to tell him so he knows before he lets Jungkook kill him, do the right thing Y/n", he begs me.

Time returned to the present moment

"What Y/n? Let's go now we find him", he looked at me.

Jimin P.o.v

How is that possible, I want her blood so much. "Go and get that blood, it's what you need, kill her if you have to", my evil side appeared. "No you love her", my good side appeared. "What has love got to do with this? You are an alpha vamp that heart can go if you just allow yourself to be one with this blood", my evil side laughed. "Don't lose yourself Jimin, she is your soulmate and if you kill her you die as well", my good side spoke. "No you'll become the strongest vampire to ever exist, you don't need her", my evil side spoke. Stop it both of you, I can decide for myself I stab myself as Y/n holds me

Y/n P.o.v

No Jimin, don't. "Y/n, let's take him home first, stop crying ok, he'll be okay", Tae carried him. Ok, thanks Tae. We make our way home. "Y/n are you ok?" Jimin asked me. Jimin you awake, I'm glad, how are you feeling? "What happened?" he asked. You don't remember what happened to you? "No I remember fighting Jk and he acknowledges me as alpha then after that all goes blank", he looks worried. There's no need to remember Jimin. "Did I hurt you?" he asked. No, we were far away from each path. "Are you sure?" he asked. Ask Tae, he's here. "Hey bro, you didn't hurt anyone than yourself, I wonder why you let Jungkook live, you were supposed to kill him?" he looks at Jimin. "Not yet, he must finish what he started, he thinks I'm weak without her blood, I'm nothing", he said. "But he knows you are the strongest in the clan", Tae looked at him. You know him, we have the last round and this time I won't intake Y/n's blood, I will do it with all my power", he looks down. "Are you sure? You know Jungkook cheats", Tae looked worried. "I'm done hurting her, it's time I leave her she safe without me", he looked at Tae feeling helpless. "No Jimin, she will tell you herself why leaving her alone is a mistake", Tae leaves. Let me just take a walk just around, I love these walks, I noticed flowers everywhere I started following the flowers to the place where there he was, as handsome as ever, his hair dark and sexy. I couldn't stop drooling over him. He noticed me and winked at me as I made my way to him, my heart beating fast and I felt weak, just his stare made me weak and I just felt thirsty for him. He made me sit on his lap. "When are you going to stop being this sexy Luna hmm, you make a man oops, vampire weak hahaha", he smirks. Hmmm just cause you know I was drooling over you, don't take advantage of it. He smirked. "I'm not doing anything you are", I kissed him. "Luna what was that for?" he smiled. You were talking too much. He kissed me back, deepening the kiss, what now Jimin? "We have to fight the last fight, I don't want your blood Luna, and I want to show the pack how strong I am", he looks at me. Ok, if you say so, I want to tell you something, but I'm tired now let's leave it for after your fight. "Sounds serious, are you sure it's ok Luna?" he looked at me. Yes, it's fine. "Let me help you", he smiled again, how I will never get tired of his smile. Tae, Jimin, where am I, someone help, I wake up chained. "No one is coming for you this time, you'll be the weapon I will use to lure Jimin into losing so calm down or you won't like what I do", Jungkook smiled. Stop it Jungkook, we know you are so weak, you are afraid Jimin will expose you, He slapped me. "Don't you dare or I'll reap you alive, you're lucky I need you to defeat Jimin, I already sent a letter", he smirked. We will see.

Jimin P.o.v

Tae, I can't find her, where is she, I can't find her scent, JK I'll kill him this time, and we have to find her, Jin appears leaving a letter, it reads:

IF YOU WANT Y/N ALIVE MEET ME AT NIGHT AT OUR GROUNDS AND SHOW HER THE REAL WEAK MONSTER YOU ARE......

JUNGKOOK

"What the hell, how could he stoop so low, Y/n has been through a lot Jimin, she needs you", he got angry. Tae, what are you hiding, I know you spill now. "She will tell you everything Jimin but just know she needs you", he looked down. If you don't tell me I ain't going and I'm your alpha so tell me NOW! "She's pregnant Jimin", He looked pained. What? How is that possible, I thought it was rare, and with me and Luna how is that possible? "She'll explain everything, let's go, for now, you have to keep her safe", Tae pleaded.

Y/n P.o.v

Jimin I love you and I'm doing this for you and I'm doing this for our baby, he arrived. "Jk, show yourself", a few people were watching, I came out looking beautiful as ever as Jungkook stands in front of me, "no not yet Jimin, he smirked, here she is Jimin, why don't you come and get her", he laughed. I removed a pin from my hair that I had dipped in a dead man's blood. I love you Jimin, I stabbed Jungkook but his eyes turn red with anger, he turns and stabbed me and everything went black, all I could think of is Jimin and my baby.

Jimin.........................No...................Y/n.

Vampire's Lust
Volume Two: Black Swan

Chapter 10

I woke up in unfamiliar surroundings, the only thing I could remember was me stabbing Jungkook and him stabbing me. W-where am I? "Thank God you are finally awake, I was about to do something", she smiles at me. Who are you? I was feeling a bit scared of her, she was very unfamiliar. "Stop panicking, I am your guide and I will assist you till we know what your full power and transformation are", she examines me. What do you mean when you say transformation? "Don't worry about it, all will reveal itself soon", she looks at me. Can I ask you something? "Yes dear, feel free", she smiles. What are you? "I am an oracle witch, I see the past and the future, what is known in your Morden time as a time-traveling witch", she looks at me. Why am I with you, where's my family, where am I? "Rest dear, I'll answer your questions later", She gives me a drink, I take it and immediately fall asleep.

Jimin P.o.v

If you don't want to be a member of the pack or you don't acknowledge me as your alpha, they all remain silent, I know Jungkook is alive but without his powers he remains hidden from us, but I believe Tae can track him, he is still our brother, you can leave, and they agree and leave. "Hey Jimin, What about Y/n what do we do?" Tae looks at me with questions written all over his face. I don't know, she lied to me, and I don't want to hear her name from this day forth, do I make myself clear Tae?, I'm dead serious about this, no more Y/n talks or what she lied, she left, we move on, that's the plan, and we still have to locate Jungkook remember don't know, she lied to me, I don't want to hear her name from this day forth. "Don't be like this, she sacrificed herself for you", he looks at me. No, she was selfish and didn't care about me, she's not the same girl I fell for, who is she? "Your soulmate", he angrily responds. No Tae, stop it and get away from me, I angrily leave avoiding hurting Tae with my anger, My heart is hurting, I don't want this heart anymore, she just left me alone, didn't she think I was strong enough to defeat Jungkook? Did she see me that weak, I feel so angry towards the thought of it, I hate you Y/n and I wish I never see you, you took away everything from me by being selfish, you killed my baby, I would have an heir, some strong enough to take over but you took that away from me, how dare you huh?. My anger turns my eyes red not blue as the guardian vampire, all I have is the urge to kill and drink blood, and I look for prey and kill, satisfying my thirst.

Y/n: P.o.v

"Hey Y/n, I'm back wake up, we need to talk, she notices tears in my eyes, wake up dear", She sprinkles water on me and I immediately wake up. Ohh sorry, I fell into a deep sleep, my eyes still looked tired. "Why were you crying in your sleep?" she cups my chin. When I was stabbed I was pregnant, I lost my baby I cry as it hurts me so much. "No, stop crying my dear, your baby lives, I prevented that from happening, you are very lucky because yes you would have lost it if he deepened the weapon but the baby is fine, what I am afraid of is what your baby will become", she smiles. No, my baby will be good, he will not be evil, he will be human, and with the power, he possesses he will use them for good and save people from monsters like Jimin and Jungkook. "Tell me, you don't love Jimin anymore?" she looks at me with a smile. No, Just the thought of it makes me want to cry. I used to think he cared for me but I was wrong, he just wanted to be an alpha vampire and I will make sure he never sees my baby, it doesn't deserve a father like him, and he never loved me. "Oh he did, he just thinks you're selfish", she looks at me. How do you know that? "I'm an oracle remember", she laughs. Ohh by the way, yes I remember, where am I? "I took you back to the old Victorian year to heal you but we leave tonight, when you get back make sure you never take this amulet off, she hands it to me. It will always watch over you Y/n, we need to protect this baby, there are people after it", she smiles. Why are you helping me? "I'm your mother's sister", she looks at me as if she was waiting for a dramatic reaction. What does that mean too? Is she a witch too? "Yes, she kept it hidden for years, when you got pregnant with a guardian vampire, all the dark oracles arose because they want to kill your child, they know how powerful and fearful it's going to be", she smiles. What? No, they can't do that I won't allow it, how long have I been gone? Is my family ok? "For a full year and yes they think you staying with Jimin, but when you go back you stay at Cresta Plaza, I prepared a room for you, it's a hotel so no one dares to trouble you", she helps me stand. I hug her, thank you so much for everything.

I awaken at the hotel looking confused at the surrounding I was not familiar with, then I noticed the amulet which made me remember everything. Thank you Aunty for bringing me safely, the amulet glows with a bright green light and I hear a knock.

Chapter 11

Why are you here? Please leave NOW! "No Y/n, I won't hurt you, please heal me, I will explain what happened", he looks at me. Why should I trust you, you almost killed me. "I know Y/n, I'll explain everything but please heal me", he pleads again. Ok, just for now, he pulls you and drinks your blood, something makes him stop. "Thank you Y/n for doing this, I know I am the last person you expected to see", I take a seat a bit far from him. Why did you come here? "Because I and you are one now, I can only live if you give me your blood, you mixed your blood with mine when we stabbed each other, and we have become one with each other", he looks down. No, we are not, can you leave? He traps me making sure, I fail to move but I push him angrily. How did I do that huh? "I told you, you got power we need to figure out, you need me", he looks at me not moving. No, I don't, I'm fine I suddenly feel tired and sleepy, and I fall into his arms as sleep took over. "Rest Y/n, we will talk later, I need to go hunting, I'm so thirsty hahaha, and I must satisfy my hunger", he leaves.

Jimin P.o.v

Why do I smell a witch? You better reveal yourself before I kill you, you are aware of who I am, before I attack, she appears in front of me. "I'm sorry, her eyes were glowing pink, but I had to come to you", she looks at me. What do you want? Her eyes return to normal, "I am Han Ji Min, oracle and holder of the moon power and I need your help as the guardian vampire", she looks at me. Hahahaha, what would a witch possibly need my help for huh? "Help me, protect Y/n", she pleads with me. Why would I want to do that, she means nothing to me. "She's carrying your hair and a lot of people are

After she and the baby, she must give birth", she looks at me. Why should I believe any word that comes from you? "Because first I'm her aunt, and second she's with Jungkook whose feeding off her and the baby, if he continues he will become even more powerful than you. I know you still love her Jimin and you know she's your soulmate, even if you deny it Jimin, she needs you to help her, protect her and take care of that baby, it's also yours", she smiles. I'll think about it and if I find out you lying, I will kill you with no hesitation. "I know, I came because I know I can't do this alone, the dark oracles have risen and are willing to kill her, think about it, and when you ready I will find you, she leaves me lost in deep thought.

Y/n P.o.v

I wake up sleeping on Jungkook's chest as he smirks looking at me, I noticed I was wearing my nightgown, and I get up panicking. "Don't worry, I didn't do anything to you except change you, I'm not saying I wasn't tempted, resisting you is very hard but I still need you", he smirks. Whatever, I make my way to the bathroom, I don't trust him, I need food why am I so hungry, an excuse to get away from him, gosh I need to feed my baby, I dress but as I go out I see Jungkook looking at me. "I'm going with you", he smirks. No. "I wasn't asking, I'm protecting you, come on give me a chance to prove myself, I've changed Y/n because of you", he smirks again. Just keep your hands of me. Yes mam, he smiles and we leave. "Let's keep a low profile, no one must see us or they will attack us", he looks at me. Are you scared Jk? "Not for me but you, I'm strong but not you hahaha", he laughs. Who told you that? "Let's race, if I win I choose what we get", he smirks. If I win? "You'll choose what you want", he smiles. That's a deal, you already race him leaving him behind, but something catches my eye as I noticed two vampires fighting a wolf-like creature, they smell me. "Well, well, what do we have here, prey tell me such nice food?" he laughs. "We gonna devour her slowly", the other one laughs. No, I was just passing through. As they get close Jungkook comes attacking them but they overpowered him. Jungkook, Nooooooo, I angrily attack one of them with all my power ripping his heart out, what have I done? Jungkook pulls you and you hold on to him as you get home, what did I do? "It's your strength, you need to let it out Y/n before it hurts you", He looks at me worriedly. What are you talking about? "You wanted to eat that heart didn't you?" he smirks. No WH.......what are you talking about? "Go and rest Y/n, we will discuss it when you feel better", he smiles at me. Ok fine, but you were hurt too, take my blood. He pulls me drinking my blood, he lets go and I go and rest *

Jimin P.o.v

"I saw them together", Tae looks at me. Who? "Kook and Y/n", he looks at me. When was this? "Today, she's not the Y/n I know", he looked at me with fearful eyes. What did you see? "She reaped out one of my guy's hearts and she looked at the heart like she wanted to eat it", he looks at me. No that's not true, you lying, Y/n would never do that, suddenly I remembered the witch and I decided to go and see her before believing what I was hearing.

Y/n P.o.v

I cry as I think of the event that just happened, who is this monster I have turned to?, how could I do something so evil like that, it's not me, suddenly I feel a cold sensation giving me goosebumps as I looked up I saw his dark eyes, his freaky hair, his scent made me quiver, he just stared at me not saying anything, desire overcame me, I wanted him so much as though it was our first time meeting, he came closer to us. "Is it true Y/n? My baby is still alive? Are you transforming?" he looked deep into my eyes.

Chapter 12

Y/n P.o.v

Where have you been Jimin huh? I have been waiting for you for a long time, you didn't even bother to look for me. "I'm sorry Y/n, I thought you killed my baby, I was angry and I was wrong to think that", he kisses me not allowing me to breathe. Jimin doesn't do this, I need time, please leave me. "Y/n, I'm sorry, please forgive me for what I did", he pleads with me. It's ok but I don't want you here, for now, please leave. "I will come for you, we have to protect that baby, make sure Jungkook doesn't find out I was here or he will harm you", he leaves. Why can't I say no to him?, every time he is around me, I feel complete, all these emotions, what must I do with them, he hurt me so badly yet I don't want him to leave, and how did he know I was supposed to be protected, all this is confusing, let me go and make some food. What must I make today? I feel cold hands touching your waist. "I need you Y/n", he whispers. Leave me alone Jungkook. "You don't understand how bad I need you", he kisses me not letting go. Stop it Jungkook, I don't want this please, I don't want to hurt you. "I want to have all of you, he makes me turn so that I face him, why can't I have you? I know you want me Y/ n, I can smell it in you", he kissed me and I kissed him back, I let go, he pulled me drinking my blood, and I slapped him. Leave me alone, I go to my room full of tears, what have I done, why did I kiss him back?, why is Jungkook doing as he pleases with me, I took out my feelings for Jimin on him, why did I kiss him back, I hate him gosh, I need to see Lisa now, how do I leave without him seeing me, can't I use my amulet, I rubbed it and called her she appeared before my eyes. "What is it my dear?" she asks. I want to go see Lisa without Jungkook noticing, I want to clear my head, please help me. "Ok my dear, but be careful, he is very cautious with you, he knew Jimin came to you and was acting out of jealousy, I'm afraid he might hurt you, you need Jimin, don't shut him out Y/n", she pleads with me. I'm not I was just going through the emotions maybe it's my hormones I don't know what to do. "Calm down my dear, go and see Lisa, after you come home, I'm sure Jimin will pay you a visit, just tell him how you honestly feel, and he'll come back to you", she puts me in a trans as I open my eyes I arrive at home seeing Lisa sitting looking lost. Lisa, I missed you so much, I hugged her. "Where have you been huh? Did you forget me?" she looks at me. I would never forget you, Lisa, I've been with Jimin, we were sorting some stuff out, and can we go eat my treat? "Ohh I'm down for that girl, I missed you so much, uncle Kai was busy, he doesn't get time to spend with me, I hate it", we get to an eatery. I know I haven't spent time with you guys, but I will, I have just been dealing with a lot my dear, I was losing myself. "What do you mean?" she looks worried. I'll tell you when I can dear, right now I just want to forget it all. As I leave Lisa's home, I make my way as I notice see Tae coming my way. "Hi Y/n", but he didn't look at me, he was filled with fear. Been a long since I saw you, I get close to him but he steps away, what is it? Why are you looking at me like that? "It's nothing, let's go I gotta get you home safe", he looks at me. If you gonna behave like this, then leave me alone, I can find my way home and I can protect myself, I start walking fast but he follows behind silently till I get home. As I enter Jungkook is nowhere to be seen. Where is he?, I'm glad he didn't notice that I left, I go to my room, I lock the door, I lay down but feel very restless, I decide to take a shower, and as I get ready to shower, I feel hairs stand as cold hands touch my tiny waist, grabbing and pulling me close. H....ey what the........ He kisses me, and I kiss him back deepening the kiss, why do I feel weak to him, he lets me go. "I'm sorry y/n", he looks at me. For what? I smirk. "For leaving you alone and not being there for my baby", he passionately kisses me. I missed you so much Jimin, so much, I kiss him back passionately biting his lips lower lip. "I missed you too Y/n, you look so pale, are you feeding my baby?" he smiles. No, right now feed me, I desire you, baby, I want you so bad, I kiss him leaving bite marks on his neck, he deepens the kiss making me moan loudly, Jimin-aaah make love to me, I need you. "Someone's in a hurry but not today I gotta feed you and my baby", he smiles. What are you talking about? "You gotta drink blood Y/n", he looks at me. No Jimin, why? "Because that baby you carrying is half vampire and half human, if you don't it will kill you", he looks at me. Are you sure, I'll be ok? "I'm here Y/n, I already got everything ready", he smirks. Ok Jimin, we go out and he makes me sit comfortably as he hands me the blood, I drank it thinking only of my baby, Jimin, I hate the taste, and do I have to do it every day? "No I'll let you know, also stop feeding Jungkook your blood, he's feeding off my baby", he looks at me with a serious.

What. "Your aunt will explain, she's really worried about you", he smiles comforting me. What about Tae, why is he acting like he's afraid of me? "Because he saw you reap that out heart out of his friend", he looks at me. No Jimin, that was no......no Jimin, I didn't mean to. "I know but we have to figure out what you becoming, the full moon is approaching, and as we get out of the room, we find Jungkook waiting, staring at Jimin with blood vengeance eyes. "Well, well, what do we have here brother, he approaches Jimin. "I'm here for her", he smirks. "Who told you she needs you?" Jungkook stares at him. "I'm here for my baby to protect them from monsters like you", he attacks Jimin with Chinese powder making him feel pain and blinding him. Jungkook, stop hurting him.

Chapter 13

"Why can't you see me Y/n, am I not strong enough for you just because I'm not an alpha anymore", he was looking scruffy and pale. Please stop it, he pushes me away as he beats Jimin till he looked half dead. "If I can't have her, you can't too Jimin", he angrily shouts. No, you won't hurt him, I stand and forcefully push him away from Jimin shielding him. You hurt him, you hurt me and you hurt my baby. "You lucky brother, next time you won't be so lucky", he smirks and leaves.

Jimin P.o.v

I sit comfortably making sure she didn't notice the pain I was in, I'm sorry Luna, I failed you both. "What do you mean by that huh?" she looks at me. I couldn't protect you at all, I don't deserve to be Alpha, and I'm weak Y/n. "No together we will protect each other, no matter what, and I love you Park Jimin", she smiles. I cough, before speaking, how much? "Take my blood, and heal Jimin then I show you", she smiles.

Han Ji Min P.o.v

Hello Sister. "How dare you?" Y/n's mom looks at me. I'm protecting her from you all. "That child must die at all costs, it will destroy us", she snarls. That is where you are wrong, you didn't see what I saw, and you know I'm stronger than you, so I will do what it takes to protect her, to protect them both. "Even dying for her?" she laughs. Hahahaha is that a threat huh? "A promise, be careful who you trust Han Ji Min, I will crush you", she threatens. She's your daughter, why do you hate her so much? "Why should I when I don't know what creature she is", she looks at me. She's not a creature but family, be careful sister, we shall meet soon as I leave.

Y/n P.o.v

I'm ok Jimin, stop worrying about me ok, the baby kicks. "You now starting to show Y/n, we have to be careful", he looks at me. Shh come feel this, I pulled his hand, and he feels the baby kick, isn't it worth protecting huh? "It is Luna", he kisses me passionately. "You know you are so beautiful Luna, Every time I stare into your eyes I see peace, something I haven't seen in decades and centuries I have existed in", he smiles. How many girls have you married since you've lived this long? "No one, I waited for you, you are mine, my soulmate Luna, that's why your blood works on me, and no other vampires, and I'm sorry I almost gave it all up for my selfish reasons", as he almost kisses me, the door breaks open. "Jimin you are needed quick", Suga rushes in. "What is it that you disturb me like this huh? He stands almost falling. He's not strong enough, what is Suga? "It's ok Y/n, I can do it, what is wrong?" I look at him. "It's Jk, he's killing all the vamps of the council, he started now, and we can't find him", he looks at Jimin avoiding my eyes. "How do you know it's him?" he questions Suga. "He left a shiny dagger with initials JK, which was laid bare, I found it in the woods dripping drops of vamps blood, and He's coming after you last as the guardian vamp", he looks worriedly. "Ok tell pack not to panic, get me Tae, you may leave", he leaves. "Already here, Tae speaks as Suga leaves. "Can the packs help since you also alpha in your territory?" he asks. "Yea, sure as long as they don't get killed, and Y/n I wanted to apologize for my behavior, no one must behave like that with a pretty Luna like you, Jimin explained everything, I'm re- ally sorry Y/n", he pleads with me. Stop saying sorry and make me food, I'm so hungry and I know you are a great cook. I need to talk to Jungkook, I know only I will be able to stop all this, and I hope I can buy Jimin time to get better. Hey Jimin, I'm taking a walk nearby, will be back now. "Ok, Y/n don't you go too far", he kisses me. I leave looking at places you once met, he pulls me close drinking my blood. "Gosh you're my life, I'm sorry I was jealous of seeing you, and Jimin I just lost my cool, I don't want to lose you Y/n, you are my everything, you know that?" he looks at me. Why are you lying, if I was, why are you killing members of the council? "They wanted to kill me, I had to fend for myself, I'm sorry Y/n", he came close to me, holding me close to him. Stop killing, and show me you have changed Jungkook, please, it's all I ask of you. "Hahahaha, I'll think about it, he kisses me and I kiss him back. No, we can't do this. "Well, well lookie, what we have here? Hello Y/n, miss me?".

Chapter 14

Sorry, who are you? Suddenly they pull Jungkook by force leaving me exposed and alone, I'm sorry, who are you? What do you want? "That child must die, we are the dark oracles and we have come to make sure that it doesn't happen". They beam a glowing light attacking and hurting me till I fell. "No Y/n, he fights so much but the hold is too strong", he winces in pain. Please don't hurt me, I don't know who you are. "We told you, and this baby must not be born, it will destroy us all", they chant words just as they are about to attack, Jimin stands in front of me being affected by the powerful force. No Jimin, please don't hurt him, they attack but he fights back his eyes turning blue killing them all. "Y/n, we have to go, he will hurt you when he is like this", Jungkook pleads. Ok, Jimin, I'll come for you, I love you, he attacks everyone not looking if I were there or not, and Jungkook smirks as he leaves holding my hand.

Jimin P.o.v

Why can't I control this power huh, I hurt those I love Evil Jimin: See your potential Jimin, YOU ARE THE GUARDIAN VAMPIRE, get rid of that heart once and for all. If I do I lose Y/n forever. "Doesn't matter, you'll be stronger than ever", my evil side appears. But what's good about that, is I'll be lonely. "But you'll be strong without your heart, you won't feel anything, no pain, no worry about anyone, just powerful and most feared amongst all, you'll rule over all", my evil side laughs. I know but I don't want to not love her, as my eyes clear, Han Ji

Min appears before me. What are you doing here? "I need your help", Han Ji Min looks at me. Why are you so interested in receiving help from me? "Only you have the power to destroy my sister", she looks. Why would I want to destroy Y/n's mom that would kill her? "You don't understand, she's not who you think she is", she looks down. Enlighten me then

Time skipped recapping year

Han Ji Min P.o.v

Sister, please don't do this. "We have to so we protect your baby", Y/n's mom looked at me. But she will never know I exist. "But she will be safe, the oracles will harm her if we don't do this, I will take care of her, if the oracles find out you slept with a vampire swan protector, they will kill you both and I can't give that up, I can't lose my sister because of this baby", she looks at me. Will you protect her? "Yes, you know I will, she's after all my niece, but she must not fall in love with a guardian vampire or have a baby with one, or dark oracles will rise and kill her, so I will protect her, you have my word sister", she smiles at me. Ok, I shall trust you with her life while I stay hidden. She leaves.

Time returned to present time

Jimin P.o.v

"You see why I must protect her, she's my daughter, I can't even tell her I'm proud of her, I'm glad she's got you and loves you that I know will keep her safe", she looks at me. How do you know that yet she's wanted dead cause of me, I almost killed her. "Because I know you can protect her, I know you love her, I searched for it once and lost it don't lose it", she leaves.

Y/n P.o.v

Who were those people Jungkook? "The ones from dark oracles, they don't mean well Y/n, but I'm happy you're safe", he smirks. Is Jimin going to be ok? "No he's not safe to be around you, he'll hurt you", he looks at me. Who are you to tell me that? I'm carrying his baby, and that changes a lot, thank you for bringing me here, I need to rest now.

"Ok go rest we will talk later", I leave and close the door, lost in thought. Why couldn't I stay and help him, I promised to work together, to keep each other safe, to keep our baby safe, seeing him like that I ran and never looked back, what is wrong with me, why do I doubt him?, I hated feeling like this. "Y/n can I come in?" he looks at me. What do you want Jungkook, it's only been two minutes. He comes close to me pulling you by the waist. "I wanted to say sorry", he kisses me, slowly and passionately, I don't let go, I deepen the kiss, kissing his neck, Jimin clears his throat, and I let go. It's not what you think.

Chapter 15

"Then what is it huh?" he looks at me. I...........Jungkook smirks and leaves, I'm sorry Jimin. "For what exactly?" he looks at me. For you to see that, it didn't mean anything. "Right, and I'm a fool to think that huh?" he looks at me. No, you don't understand Jimin Please. "Then make me understand", he was now getting angry. I can't but I'm very sorry. "Yeah me too, he pushes me aside as he leaves. Jimin, please don't leave, I hold onto him tightly not letting go. "Let me go now", he tries fighting. No, I can't let you leave me Jimin. "Isn't you got JK, he will protect you", he fights but my grip was way too strong, he was failing. No Jimin, you not leaving us alone this time. "You can't make me stay you lying hoe, leave me alone, I don't have to talk anymore, if it wasn't for the baby you carrying we wouldn't be talking", he pushes me hard making me fall hard-hitting the wall which was behind you, everything went black.

Jimin P.o.v

Why is she lying to me? What have I done to her for her to hurt me like this? I shed tears, my heart is so heavy, and I feel so much pain at her betrayal, doesn't she feel the same about me huh ?, if I can't win over Jk then I will give up everything and let the Calvary end me for good, doesn't she know I live for her, she's my life and I want my baby safe. Tae comes sitting next to me and pulls me hugging me. "Bro, take it easy, it's not what you think or how you perceive it", he tries to console me. Then how am I supposed to think huh? I saw them kissing each other passionately, and you say it's not what I think, you all think I'm a fool right? "No Jimin, calm down, she will explain it", he looks at me. What's there to explain? You know how much it kills me just the same as it killed you with Rose, you understand me now brother? I stand vigorously turning away from Tae, I have decided to give myself to the Calvary because without her being mine, I have no reason to live, I'll see you later Tae, and I leave.

Y/n P.o.v

Jimin wasn't supposed to see that, did Jungkook do it on purpose?, he knew Jimin would see, how could I have been selfish and blind, I wanted to keep him from killing Jimin, and he knew the only thing that would hurt him was seeing that the thought of it makes me angry. "Hey Y/n, can we talk?" he looks at metal about what exactly? "I'm glad he saw that, at least I don't have to hide how I feel for you anymore", he smirks. What do you mean? "I like you, you my prey, and I will protect you, and you don't need Jimin", he smirks again. Who are you to decide that for me huh? so you made him see that on purpose, did you see how it hurt him, stay in your lane Jungkook I'm not afraid of you anymore, but if you ever pull a stunt like that, I will kill you myself, better hope Jimin comes around because if he doesn't I'll be the one to end you. "I would like to see you try, he kisses my lips, so sweet and so pure", I slap him and leave.

Jimin P.o.v

Jimin: Why do I smell her scent near me? No Jimin leave her, end this desire, fuck my feelings, I'm just so sick of this. All my brothers have kissed her, how sick is that?

Y/n P.o.v

I got to the place where Jimin was, he looked pale and lank, but he made my blood run Icy cold, he brought shivers to my knees. Can we talk? "Yeah sure", he pulls me close to him making me sit on his lap. I'm sorry Jimin for.....he kisses me deeply making my lips swell. "I hate Jk touching you, I'm sorry I left just like that, I'm sorry I doubted you", he looks at me.No you shouldn't be apologizing Jimin, please forgive me, I thought if I do it Jk would stop all the killing and won't hurt you. "I know Y/n, I'm guardian vampire, but if I can't have you, I'll surrender myself to the Calvary known as the aurimary clan, always remember that", he kisses me lightly. No Jimin, you can't, why would you think that? You can't leave us alone, if you do that, then I will do the same, you can't leave us, he doesn't say anything just kisses me passionately, deepening the kiss just as I was about to say something, everything went black.

Chapter 16

Jimin P.o.v

Y/n wake up, why isn't she waking up? I rush her to a hospital only known to our kind. Hi Jin, please may you help me, she's pregnant, and he quickly attends to her. "Can we talk? He looks at me worriedly. Yeah is she ok? Is my baby ok? "Yes, they are both fine, but I'm worried the baby is breaking her bones Jimin, she's not feeding properly, look after her, these last days will be hard for her, don't tell her how the baby is killing her, she might not take it well", he pleads with me. But Jin, she has to be ok, I can't lose her. "Then be the man she needs, support her, feed her your blood, it's the only way she'll become stronger", he looks me dead in the eye. But it will weaken me. "But you have to save her, choose what's important, think about it, she's up, and was asking for you", he smiles. Are you sure she will be fine if she feeds off me? "Yes, it will strengthen her", he looks at me assuring me. Then I'll do it, I would do everything for her. I leave to see her.

Y/n P.o.v

Where is he? I hate being alone, He enters startling me, his gaze was making me feel numb and dumbfounded, I couldn't even say anything, he looked so attractive. "Hi Luna, how are you feeling?" he smiles. Where have you been? I was now feeling lonely. "I was having a word with the doctor", he sits next to me. Is everything ok with our baby? "Yes Luna, don't worry a lot, it's not good for the baby, Luna will you be ok feeding off me? I don't want you to do something you are not comfortable with", he looks at me seriously. What do you mean to feed on you? "For the baby to live you have to drink my blood, it will strengthen you", he smiles. But weaken you? I can't do that. "You have to, to save our baby", he kisses me this time it was light and pale not usual. What's wrong Jimin? "You have to stay with me till our baby is born, I don't want you seeing JK, he's the one who weakens you and our baby Luna", he rays my hair. Ok Jimin, but first get me outta here, I go get some of the stuff I need then we go. We leave. I get my stuff ready to leave while Jimin waits out, Jungkook comes in and closes the door, locking it. What are you doing? I don't want to see you right now. He pulls me by the waist while sucking my blood. Leave me alone, I'm leaving. "Not yet, you'll do as I say or I kill you right now", he holds me tightly. Then Jimin will kill you if you do that. "Try me, he doesn't even know what's happening now hahahahahaha tears my dress leaving me exposed with just my panty and bra. Jungkook, what the hell are you doing, please leave me alone, I'm leaving. He kisses me everywhere leaving very red bite marks. "What's wrong Y/n, am I not man enough for you, don't you want me huh, was it all fake? ", he slaps me whilst kissing me. Jungkook, please leave me alone. "Why? I also want you so bad, YOU MINE, not Jimin's, and today you will know that", he pushes me onto the bed locking my hands and making sure I couldn't move as he forced himself on me, bruising me, raping me, tears fell as I felt the pain and I couldn't even scream, my thighs were bruised every part of my body was bruised. Leave me alone. "I'm sorry Y/n, I don't know what came over me", he looks at me shaking. Leave me alone, I wear my dress as I leave, no

Emotion came from me, I was numb. "Y/n, where have you been, was starting to worry", Jimin asks. All I did was cry my heart out, he noticed the marks on me. Who did this? Can we go home please, I limp as I get inside the car, it was crushing me seeing him hurt like that, and the ride was silent till we got home? Thank you for everything. I cry, he overpowered me, did as he pleased, and raped me. I cry hard. He stood there emotionless with no words coming from him, who did this Y/n? Was it Jungkook? I will kill him if it's him", he looks at me. Can I go lie down? He carries me softly. "We will talk when you wake up, sleep. "I just turn away hugging myself, not facing Jimin, as I cry hard till my eyes became swollen, puffy,

    and blood red.

Chapter 17

Jimin P.o.v

Tae, I'm going out and will be back, please take care of her for me, I left some blood for her to intake, make sure she takes it. "Why do you look so pissed, Jimin what happened?" he looks at me. I don't wanna talk about it, I smash my hand on the wall making it bleed. "I've never seen you like this, what happened Jimin huh?" I just leave without saying anything

Y/n P.o.v

I wake up feeling so much pain, I manage to take a shower and wear something comfortable, how could Jungkook do that? I couldn't even fight him, it will kill Jimin if he finds out, what do I do? "Hey Y/n, can I come in, how are you feeling?" Tae comes next to me. Yea, I'm better. "Before we talk, what happened?" I hug him not saying anything. "I can't help you if you don't talk to me", he looks at me. I'm sorry Tae and thank you for being here. "What got Jimin so angry?" he rays my hair comforting me. J...Jungkook raped and abused me. "He did what? Did you tell Jimin?" he looks at me. No, I was scared and confused, please take me to the doctor, my baby Tae, please help me, we will deal with Jimin later before he kills Jungkook. "Ok hurry up, get on my back", I do so and we rush.

Jimin P.o.v

I will kill whoever touched and hurt my Luna. "What if it's Jungkook, will you kill your brother huh?" my good side appeared.

Yes, he touched my woman and I hate it. "Don't forget the law Jimin, brother can't kill brother", my good side reminded me. I know so I must leave it, no can't do that, I will however hunt Jungkook now, I search for hours but find nothing. You can hide but I'll find you eventually don't think I can't, I can kill you as alpha, you don't deserve to even exist Jungkook, how dare you touch my Luna, you put my baby in danger, even if I don't agree I know it was you, how could I have been so selfish, leaving Y/n, and alone with a monster like you. I keep searching.

Y/N P.O.V

"We have a problem, we have to operate y/n, and the codes are choking the baby", Jin looks at me worriedly. But it's still a fetus "Did you see your scan dear, your baby has grown even though it's not showing yet, it's a vampire-mixed baby remember, if not we have to induce immediate vomiting and surgery we remove the codes killing the baby", he looks at me worried. "Do everything you can to save them both, I'll get Jimin", Tae panics. "It could go sideways", Jin says looking very worried. "Save them both doctor, I don't care what it costs, even my soul and blood, just save them, please. "We will try our best, you have to get Jimin here, she needs his blood and she needs him more than ever", he pleads with Tae. "I hope I make it on time Jin", Tae holds my hand before leaving. "It's ok, we put her to sleep so she doesn't feel pain, go NOW!!!!!!!" he pleads with me angrily.

Jimin P.o.v

I take a seat. I will kill him, as I smell Jung kook's scent, I dodge the dagger, he threw at me, not today brother, how dare you rape her huh? "You can't have it all Jimin, I'll take it all from you, I know how good she tastes now hahahahahaha", I attack him vigorously, making him bleed. I'm still alpha, no matter what you do, I should have killed you, you don't deserve life, just death, and this time I will show you no mercy. "We will see you soon weak Alpha, we shouldn't have been brothers", he spits out blood. One thing we both can agree on I beat him up badly almost killing him, Tae stops both of us. Leave me now before you also get hurt, stop trying to be a good guy Tae, and did I not ask you to look after Y/n? "Why do you think I'm here, you need to go to her, there's a problem, stop all this now, Jungkook is to blame for everything, I know but she needs you Jimin", he looks at me worriedly. What's wrong Tae, you looked fearful, did she attack you again? "Just go to her Jimin NOW!!!!! Because she's fighting for her life and your baby's life"

Chapter 18

What do you mean huh? "Doc said one might survive and now is not the time for you to fight Jungkook, we will deal with him later, the pack will put him in the dungeons, go Jimin, don't waste time here, she needs you", I leave. Jin how is she? Can I see her? "Ok, but for now don't tell her how critical she is", he looks at me. Will she be ok? "Let's hope so, because whoever raped her made sure the baby's code was choking", he shows me the scan. Do you mean he was trying to kill the baby? "Yes, the only way to do that was to sexually force himself into her breaking a code that linked them together", anger arose in me. I will kill him, who is he working for, this is not Jungkook, I will need answers, save them both, and I'm counting on you. "Ok go see her, then leave we get operating, but if it goes sideways we will have to induce premature labor and then incubate the baby till it's fully grown, but if we do you'll have to feed it the whole three days it will weaken you", he looks at me again. I'll do it if need be I leave and make my way to her.

Y/n P.o.v

"Hey Luna, how are you feeling", he rays my hair. I'm ok Jimin, where have you been? "Just clearing my head, I don't like what Jungkook did, I wanted to kill him but couldn't, his my brother after all", he looks at me. How did you know it was him, I never told you. "He's my brother Y/n, one thing he can never do is hide things from me", he smiles at me but I could tell something was eating him up. I'm sorry. "For what Luna, shh no apologizing, get strong, drink my blood

Luna, it's for the baby", he smiles. I hate how it tastes, it also weakens you Jimin: But I will do it for you and our baby. Han Ji Min appears in front of us. "Sorry to come like this, we have to go, Y/n will die, After Jungkook raped her, and he left witches tracking on her we have to leave now", she looks at us. "Won't they suspect or follow her where we go? "That's where you come in, Smear your blood on the bed, your blood will put off the witch", she still keeps her eyes on us. But he's weak aunty. "Why would he be weak Y/n, he can do it he's a guardian vampire", she smiles. Because.......Jimin smoothers blood everywhere, I feel light all of a sudden everything whirls and turns black. I wake up finding Jimin Staring at me, yet his gaze never left me. Why are you looking at me like that Jimin? "Cause I'm lucky to have you, and I will do everything in my power to protect you", smiling at me, he comes closer. Then don't leave me alone. "I won't Y/n, someone gotta keep you company", he winks at me making me blush a little. "Sorry to disturb you but I need to check Y/n, I want to see if the code has moved but first she has to feed", she smiles. "You know what to do Luna", he smiles. Yes, I grabbed his hand close to my lips and drank his blood, but this time the thirst was more, and stopping was hard. "Stop Y/n, you killing him, find the will to stop", I looked into his eyes which were turning pale, and I stopped. Jimin, I'm sorry, I couldn't find the will. "It's ok, it's the baby Y/n, not you, it will strengthen you", he passes out. Aunty, please help him, it's my fault he passed out, and Tears roll down my cheeks

Tae P.o.v

Yeah, Jungkook let's talk I need answers, why did you rape Y/n like that? "Because that stupid witch promised me to be alpha, but she couldn't keep her word", he angrily hits the wall. Why do you hate Jimin so much? "He got all guardians power, he doesn't deserve Y/n", he sits down angrily. Does that mean hurt her? I told you that witch told me to do it", he smirks. Which witch? "Y/n's mom", he looks at me. What ...that can't be true why would she want Y/n and her baby dead? "Because Y/n is the descendent of the black swan power and her mom possesses the power of the moon", he doesn't move his gaze from me. No, her aunt possesses that power. "You stupid fool, Y/n's mom is the aunt, and Han Ji Min is the mom, she is the one protecting her because I didn't want to harm her", he looks down. Why wouldn't you huh? "Because I have feelings for her", he looks down.

Chapter 19

Aunty why is he still not up, tears fall. "He will be ok Y/n, stop crying, it's not good for the baby", she smiles at me. Please may you leave us, I want to try, and wake him up. You know, I blush, failing to tell her. Hahaha, it's ok dear, take your time, I'm going out and will be back later", she leaves. Hey Jimin, wake up, I need you, As I kissed him not noticing he was kissing me back, I stopped and looked at him as he stared back at me, full of desire, and lust, he wanted me like I was his prey. Jimin, you awa......he smashes his lips against mine deepening the kiss, leaving my lips rosy pink and swollen, he pulls my neck kissing it leaving visible marks, my moans were his ecstasy, his drug, he wanted me even more not stopping himself. "I want you Y/n, let me feel you", he kissed my neck. Do as you please, he smirked at the way I was obeying his dominance, he kisses me not allowing me to breathe, making me moan as I was now so turned on...Jimin ahhhhhhhhhh

Tae P.o.v

You what? "I have feelings for her, and I will stop at nothing to make her mine", he looks at me. She doesn't feel the same. "If she didn't why she kiss me back, not once but five times, she wants me, you're just jealous cause you wanted her but couldn't grab her, you're so weak, Rose didn't want you so you rapped her. Hahahaha, will y/n like you when she finds out "I leave with anger and bitterness in my head, Y/n's mom appears before Jung kook's eyes. "How did you fail such a simple task, you got your pleasure what about our deal huh? Should I kill you now?" she looks at Jungkook angrily. Before she chants, Tae wounds her with witch-killing bullets, which will paralyze her for some time. have questions, I need answers from you. "You can't keep me here for long", she laughs. I can tell me what I want to know.

Y/n P.o.v

I'm glad you feeling better, I smirk. "What is that smirk for huh?" he looks at me. Because I made you feel better. "Who told you it was you", he smirks. Want me to show it again? I pin him on the bed locking him, as I kissed him passionately not allowing him to breathe, knock breaks the kiss as you laugh about it. It's ok aunty, you can come in. "Sorry to bother you, but you guys have a visitor, but it's not good news", she looks down worriedly as Tae appears from behind Her. "I'm sorry Jimin it's y/n's mom and Jk", he looks at Y/n. My mom, what did she do huh? She tried to end JK for failing to kill you and the baby", he looks down. What? Why would she want to kill me huh? No that's a lie, tears fall, stop lying. "I'm not, why don't you ask Jimin, huh, Jimin say something, we wasting time", Tae pleads to him. "Let's go now Han, stay with her please", he kisses me. We arrive at the dungeons and find both of them missing. "Where are they?" Jimin searches. We are here, we've been waiting for you, they threw ropes with chines powder mixed with blood, which made all guardian vampires so weak, I couldn't even move. "What took you so long, we were starting to think you not coming hahaha", she laughs. Jungkook was not saying anything as the hex bags were controlling him to follow her every command. "Right now we have bait, we need Y/n, I'm sure she will come for him hahaha, humans are so pathetic they get fooled easily worse when they are in love, they become confused stupid little things", she laughs. "Is that why you never had anything good, you were jealous of your sister, she was always one step ahead of you. She attacks him angrily this time. "She wasn't", she laughs. "Then why is she behind you?" she turns to see Han Ji Min, who blinds her severely with witch-mixed incense. "You think you can harm my daughter, sister when I'm still alive? NEVER!!!!!!!

Chapter 20

What do you mean daughter huh? "Y/n now is not the time for questions, help Jimin, hurry, if you don't he will die, it's crushing his bones", she looks at me. What am I supposed to do? How do I help him? "Take him to a near river, and wash him, make sure you don't get out till his eyes turn blue", she hugs me. Ok, I hurry to help Jimin to his feet, Please be ok Jimin, he wasn't saying anything except growling in pain, We were almost there, as we noticed the river, Han mentioned, we entered the water, washing him as I remembered the kiss he gave me when I had fallen once, and I did the same, his eyes turning blue immediately, we got out of the water coughing, Are you ok?. "You saved my life, you forget you are pregnant, you risked your life how I could be ok huh?" he looks at me. You're worth it remember, this baby is strong like its father, so I wasn't worried about it.

Han Jin Min P.o.v

"What have you done, I could have ended everything, you are a selfish sister", Y/n's mom spits blood. Why would you want to kill my baby, after all, why did you raise her, if you were going to kill her huh? I look at her angrily. "Because I didn't know, she would be foolish enough to fall in love with a vampire", she looks down in pain. What is wrong with that huh? "It always destroys families look at what happened to us, I lost my sister to that monster, and all I wanted was my sister back, I thought if I took the one thing that separated us I would have you back", she looks at me. Well, it doesn't change, I hate you for trying to kill my baby sister, this is the end, I kill her, goodbye sister, it all stops. "No mom, Aunty you killed my mom why", tears fall. She hugs me. It had to be done, my dear. "Let go of me, I don't want to see you", she looks at me. Don't raise your voice, I'm your mother, whether you like it or not. "You are not my mother, you are a monster, get away from me, tears fall hard as she mourned the death of her mother, and her strength arose in her turning her eyes black. You have transformed my daughter.

Y/n P.o.v

I'm not your daughter, I push her away, and Jimin tries to calm me down. "No Y/n, I can't you'll hurt the baby, I push him away, and get away from me, Han starts moving in fear, how dare you kill her huh? I grab her by the throat, and Jimin pulls me. No, I push him stabbing him with the knife I wanted to use on Han, Jimin NOOOO! "It's the only way, as he loses power. Why did you do that, I told you not to be involved huh, why? "It's ok Y/n, that good in you mustn't live you, take care of our baby, I will always be there for you in your heart", he smiles at me. Noooo Jimin, don't say that, don't die on me, please. "I love you Y/n, my Luna, My Soul, take care of yourself", he passes out. What have I done, No Jimin please, I stood there, frozen, paralyzed by fear and guilt, and I don't want to live without you. Jimin, Please wake up, I kept looking at his pale body. "Y/n, can we talk?" Jungkook pulls me up. What the hell do you want huh, he smirked, and you're the reason he's here. "You did that yourself, but if you want I can bring him back", he smirks. What? What do you want in return? "Be my eternal wife, then he lives, I'll give you a few minutes to think about it, so what's it going to be huh?" he smirks. Do IT, I'll marry you if it saves him, please I'll do anything, before he does anything Tae comes running. "No y/n, Jimin is not dead just in a Trans, don't listen to Jungkook", he looks at me. Jimin, Don't do that to me, wake up from whatever this is, Jungkook why would you lie to me like this huh? can't you see how much this hurts me just as you cry you feel your tummy aching so much? Ouch my baby, Help me please as I felt an excruciating pain noticing blood dripping from your thighs. Noooo my baby please help me Tae. He quickly carries me not looking back and takes me to Jin. "Please be ok Y/n I can't lose you too please save them Jin, please", Tae pleads. Be alright my baby, please you can save your father only you can bring light to his life, the one I couldn't bring to him as you black out.

Tae P.o.v

"Hey Tae we managed to save both the baby and Y/n, But there's something you have to see", he looks at Me. thank you Jin for doing your best. "They are both strong, Tae no one would come out of this but come see them, Y/n was asking to see a familiar face", he looks at me. Ok Jin thank you once more, I hope Jimin can come and see this, I know he's the strongest of his kind but this one was too deep I am worried how Y/n will take it if he doesn't come out of it...

Y/n P.o.v

Nurse when will I see my baby??? Is my baby ok? "Yes dear, He's perfectly fine and strong enough." she smiles at me. It's a baby boy oh my, I couldn't hold the tears. I wish Jimin was here to see this and share this with me I cry. "No Y/n don't do that to yourself it's a good time to laugh and be happy ok, no more crying", Tae smiles at me. I am so glad to see you, what will happen to Jimin? Will he be ok? what if Jungkook kills him? tears fall again. "Noooo Y/n don't do that to yourself you have to be strong enough remember you have to feed the baby, It will require Jimin's blood and your milk to grow stronger, Jimin had prepared about 8 bags that should be enough for now", he smiles at me. Why do you say that like he's gone, is he gone Tae? "Why don't you ask him yourself", he smirks. What do you mean Tae huh? "Hie Luna", He didn't look like the Jimin I knew, he was handsome, dark, and contagious, looking at me like I was his prey, I couldn't move or speak my body was numb, and emotions took over me.

Vampire's Lust
Volume Three: The Final Chapter

Chapter 21

Looking at him, my heart felt at ease, knowing he was with me. "Hey Tae, How was your day?" I greeted him, smiling at his handsome box smile. "Not good, I didn't get enough hunt, the pack was annoying today", he said. Enough about me Y/n, he looked up at me, how was your first day at work? I wasn't able to focus Tae, I missed Miyeon so much, it hurt, I replied. Truthfully it did hurt so much, being away from my son, it was Kinda my first day spending it without my boy. He smiled at me again, "come on Y/n, you know I take care of him don't you think?" he said. Tae, truly I am grateful for all you have done for me, I know you take care of my baby well, you've always been there, even when Jimin bailed on me and the baby, you've just been so great towards me. I truly don't know how I would have raised Miyeon by himself, where would I be getting the blood? "Speaking of Miyeon, Where is he? I asked. "I just put him to sleep, you know for a half-breed that nickel can outrun me, you know", he said. It's good for you Tae, seeing that you are also a half-breed, I wink at him. Let me go freshen up, what you say tonight we watch movies, I really could use some relaxation time, I believe mother Y/n earned it today, and he laughs. "You know I've always been down for that girl, I also need that too", he replies winking at me. Gosh it's been long time since I felt at home and free, I believe I deserve some me time once or twice, I soak myself in the bath as I relax, getting out was a dread, if I was alone would have probably fallen asleep in there, damn Tae.

Jimin P.o.v

Ok everyone listen up, I stood there as authoritatively as I could, knowing how much the pack feared me, it was salvatory for me to savor the moments. From now on, everyone reports to Jungkook, we have made peace as brothers, and have decided to work together for the betterment of the pack. We have to end the Baltimore pack, they make all breeds very bad, I want all of them killed, no mercy, I have developed new ways in which you all can be able to use and torture them you are interrogating them. Jungkook will fill you in, but if you do not follow my words as Alpha, I will end you to myself, Jungkook, a word alone as we left to our private room leaving them in whispers and questions. The room we normally carried out our talks had the old Victorian era feel because of its carpets and floral dark patterns that could make any vampire look like that idiot Dracula. "Jungkook looked at me, Sup brother? Is everything alright where are we hitting tonight?" he said. Tonight you are in charge brother, I want to go meet my son, I believe it's time now, I can feel his strength and he's starting to feed off me. He looked at me with doubtful eyes, "what about Y/n?" he asked. "What about her?" I asked in such a manner that could tell I already knew the answer to that question. "How will you face her?" he asked. I don't care about her, I only want my son, he has to be the new alpha as stated by our laws, otherwise, no one will lead this pack and it will become clan-less. The other reason is the fact that after my reincarnation, my focus is to groom the next alpha before I am killed by the Aurimary clan, I know they will end me if I don't abide by our laws as vampires. "What about your feelings for her?" he asked. I pushed him angrily, enough Jungkook, enough about her, know your place, I am your alpha too, acknowledge me, as I took a seat down a huge sigh, as I knew deep in my heart my feelings for her would never end. Come on Jimin, don't forget I am also your brother, where is Tae? I can't feed off his aura, He looked at me with talking eyes. "Me too, it's like I can't feel or see him, he went mia on us, why?" I replied and asked him. Where the hell is he?

Why is he in hiding? Especially with us, he does that when he knows he is hiding something, especially from the Aurimary clan. "Shall we search for him?" he asked. No, I quickly responded, I know he will slip up eventually, no matter how much he hides, for now, let's focus on the task at hand, going there tonight, I want to be able to see my precious son, I do want that indeed.

Y/n P.o.v

Hey Tae, I'm visiting Lisa and uncle Kai, I believe this visit is long overdue, can you watch Miyeon, I'll try and be back before evening. "Yeah, sure, but can I ask you something," he looked deep into my eyes. "Do you still love Jimin?" he asked me looking at me deep in the eyes. Where is this all coming from? "Is that a yes or a no?" he angrily looked at me. First, tell me why you have never mentioned him before. He angrily pushes me till my back hit the wall, placing a kiss on my lips and I deepened the kiss following his rhythm which made him stop. "Y/n was is wrong in me huh?, I've been with you till I fell in love with you, protecting you is the only thing I want, you my Rose and not anyone's, don't deny it, you feel the same, when I'm around you I feel the urge to touch you". He kisses me deeper not leaving any space between us, the kiss lasted for about 5 minutes. No Tae, we will talk about this when I come back, please understand, I need to clear my mind, and then I'll be able to give you a proper answer. "You just did, but I think I'll feel better hearing it from these sweet plumpy lips of yours", he smirks and touches my swollen lips not saying anything. Thank you for watching Miyeon, I know you hate it when I keep saying thank you but I appreciate it. He just smirked and winked at me as I left, geez the arrogance of this half-breed.

Getting to uncle Kai's house made my heart beat faster than I could imagine, I wonder how this will go, I don't even know how to explain all this, Jimin you piece of trash. "Hey Y/n, It's been so long we thought you forgot us, especially when we heard aunty passed away, so sorry my dear but I'm glad you're here right now", Lisa jumped and hugged me filled with joy. It's okay dear, I've just been busy and everything just happened fast, I am truly sorry for disappearing from you. 'Tell me something, what happened between you and Jimin? She paused and looked at me. "You two still together or what? I have missed so much of your life", she looked at me. That my dear is a long story but to cut it short, congratulations on being an aunt... "Wait, wait..... You mean baby?" she asked looking shocked. Yes, but Jimin left me, I have no idea where he went, Miyeon is now 2 years old, he's just a sweet boy, I'm sure you guys will love him. Please don't tell uncle Kai yet, this might hurt him so much, it just has to come from me only. "Hurt who?" uncle Kai looked at us. Hi uncle, how have you been, I'm so happy to see you, I missed you so much, I hug him not letting go. "I'm okay, how have you been? I got so worried when I didn't see you at your mother's funeral, we heard she died on your hands", he said. I wanted to come but due to my condition I couldn't, I was giving birth that day. "what? you gave birth and didn't bother telling us, let alone your sister Rose, who's in hospital, by the way, she almost took her life cause of you, and you were busy out there having fun", he slapped me. Silence rose between us but anger stirred inside me, it's not like I was having fun, where were all of you when she died in the first place, you know what coming here was a mistake, I left filled with tears and a broken heart. How could uncle say that about me, I wish they had an idea what I was truly going through, how broken I was losing Jimin, I was so broken and by the way, it's not easy raising a child by yourself working and not knowing whether he's going to be a monster or human. How dare he slap me, let me call Rose I get over this and find out what the problem is and just maybe she'll leave the hospital, I dial her number, it rings——it rings———it rings————-she finally picks up. "Hello, who is this?" she replies. It's me Y/n, your little sister. She grew silent. Rose, I'm truly sorry for not being there for you, I'm truly sorry for mom dying, it's all my fault. "How dare you leave me like that Y/n? I thought something happened to you, you chose that boy over us, right? So leave me the fuck alone, don't ever call me unless you are dying, I....... I don't have a little sister", she cuts the call. W...why did she do that? Tears just poured out my eyes like a flooded river, till my eyes became sore. You know what let me go home maybe my son will cheer me not maybe he definitely will cheer me, after all, he's all I have, all I will fight for, to heck with everyone.

Upon arriving home, Miyeon ran so fast seeing my arrival. Hi baby, I'm so happy to see you, why are you crying baby? Where is uncle Tae sweetie? He looked at me, "he said he'll be back mommy he went hunting". Ok my dear, did you eat? " Yes mommy, uncle Tae gave me some food before leaving, but mommy why are you crying so much, your eyes are big and red? " he asked looking at me. A knock interrupts us, how grateful I was for that knock at least I wouldn't have to answer my baby. Miyeon, go to your room, I find out who it is, and I'll come and get you. He runs leaving me to open the door but my eyes couldn't believe who it was. I just stood there frozen, confused, and lost.

Chapter 22

Words could not explain how I felt, seeing him in front of me, I just stood there motionless, there was nothing I wanted to say to him except bomb him with a lot of questions. "Hie Y/n", He said avoiding my eyes. What the hell are you doing here? "I want to meet my son", he said. What the hell makes you think you have the right to see him huh? "He's feeding off my Y/n, I'm not here to give an explanation for why I left or why I want to see him but I'm asking you for permission to meet my son", he pleaded, his eyes looking very desperate, making you want to forgive him and forget the hurt. Ok fine, please wait while I explain this to him, or he won't take it well, I can give you a few minutes that's all I can offer, I just left without looking at him. Thoughts surrounded my head and heart, was it right to allow him to see his son, or was I wrong? "Mommy, I'm here, what's the matter, today mommy? Why are you so sad?" he asked. I'm ok baby, Listen, I would like you to meet your father today, and "he's here? He quickly asked. Yes, baby, I can see you so excited to meet him lets go. Emotions took over when Jimin saw him, embracing him with such love and care not letting him go.

Jimin P.o.v

Hello, my son, I looked at him feeling so emotional, how handsome he was. "Hi daddy, I'm Miyeon in case mommy didn't tell you, see she forgets a lot, he giggles. I'm Jimin, I'm just so happy to see you Miyeon. "Where have you been daddy? You didn't come to see me once", he looks at me with his goggle eyes that were the same as his mother's. That my son I will explain when you are older, but just know you are the reason I am alive, I'll explain everything but for now, I have to leave, the hurt was killing me I just left without looking at Y/n.

Y/n P.o.v

Tears just fell, I was failing to control them, how could he just leave without saying anything to me? I'm sorry my baby for not telling you about your father as Miyeon came running. "Mommy stop crying, please or you'll go sick, and I kinda knew him, 'cause we share a bond which allows me to feel what he feels", he said cupping my cheeks. Why didn't you tell me about you feeding off him baby huh? "I was afraid you'll think I'm a monster", he said looking down. Hey, look at me, you are not a monster and you never will be, the one who is a monster is your father. "Ok mommy, I love you". Go and sleep my baby, I'll see you in the morning, he runs off to bed and falls asleep immediately.

Jimin P.o.v

Meeting my son went not how I expected because just seeing them both brought feelings I have been suppressing all these years, I couldn't even look at her. "Hey, so what will you do about", before he could finish anger just overtook me, nothing, my son is still young, once he's old enough I will train him, no one will dare to stop me not even Y/n. " Calm down Jimin, you know what happens when you are like this", he said trying to calm me down. LEAVE ME ALONE NOW!" Fine, I'll leave just don't do anything you'll regret," he leaves. I'm so sorry Y/n, I just hate seeing her so broken yet she's raising my son for me, I wish she knew just how much I love her, but I can't, not even to be with her, it's the only way I can keep them alive even after I die. I just want her to be happy even if it's not with me that's how much I give a fuck about her cause she's all that matters to me, let me go hunting at least that will keep my mind preoccupied and not hurt like this.

Y/n P.o.v

"Hey Y/n, why are you crying like this? What happened?" he asked looking worried. They all shut me out, Rose shut me out, I can't believe she even said I'm dead to her, the thought of it makes me cry Tae, my heart can't take all this. "They will understand Y/n......don't worry", he said looking at me. I'm sorry I forgot to tell you, but Jimin was here, just saying that caused his expression to grow darker than I thought. "What the hell did he want huh?" he asked in a loud tone. To see Miyeon, he didn't even look at me Tae, I was nothing to him, and how could he just forget everything? "See he doesn't love you, just forget him, and be happy". I know Tae, calm down please, I hate it when you like this, and he just leaves angrily.

Jimin P.o.v

"Jimin I've been looking for you", he said looking angry. Where have you been Tae? We've been searching for you everywhere. "None of your business, I found a place to call home, not you, you not my family", he said. Tae, why are you acting like this huh? You guys are the only family I have. He punched me so hard that I fell. "Listen, stay away from us, stay away from Y/n, she's been through a lot of cause of you, stop hurting her Jimin, I'm sick of this, and I'm sick of you, cleaning up after you," he punched me again making me bleed but I did not beat him or anything. Leave me now Tae, I'll hurt you, GO! He left angrily. Why is he like this, my eyes started turning, easy Jimin, stop you'll hurt the wrong people, I calmly close my eyes and took a breath counting down 5......4.......3......2...........1..........0, My eyes stopped turning and I controlled myself.

Y/n P.o.v

"Mommy, when will I see my daddy again? Miyeon asked. I don't know, he will come to you, my dear. "Why didn't you tell me about him before?" he asked. Because you were still a baby, and you still my wise baby, he yawns and I put him to sleep. I made my way to the kitchen, preparing something to eat as hunger was overtaking me, but before I could Tae came before me "I'm sorry for leaving like that, I didn't want to say hurtful words to you, I was just confused", he said looking at me. I understand but don't worry Tae, I'm over Jimin, and his expressions today showed he doesn't love me anymore. "What are you saying Y/n?" he asked. I'm tired of always being hurt, the tears, you've been there for me for three years, and I'm grateful, how would I have raised Miyeon by myself? "You're a good mother Y/n, he's lucky to be your son", he said. I'm the lucky one, so what I'm saying is make me forget Jimin, I moved closer to him, so close I could feel his breath on my skin. "Hmmm Y/n, are you okay? You haven't wanted this, just because he comes you now want this, are you using me as are bound to forget Jimin?" he asked. I kissed him not letting go, you are not rebound Tae, it's time I try and move on, and come on three years is a long time to make you rebound, I'm not saying I'll forget you if Jimin comes back, I'm saying I want to be with you as long as you want me. "Are you sure Y/n, are you sure about this?" he asked pulling me closer to him. I thought about it and yes I am sure, it will take time but I'm sure. He pulled me and kissed me not letting go, not allowing any room between us. "Please go with me to the ball Y/n, the whole pack is going to be there, and they would love to meet you, what do you say to that?" he asked.

Chapter 23

J imin P.o.v

Everyone, listen up, today must go as planned, make sure everyone behaves, if they misbehave kill them instantly, and show no mercy. If you do not abide by my words as your alpha, I'll kill you myself, this ball happens once, so enjoy yourselves but behave, Jungkook a word alone, they all leave leaving you two. "Hey, why are you looking so pale and angry Jimin huh?" he asked. It's Tae." You saw him?" he asked looking worried. Yes, he's not the same, he came to see me, threatening me to leave Y/n alone, I don't want anything to do wither, she has my son, and that's the bottom line that matters to me only. "Leave that, and focus on tonight, we will look into what Tae is planning later", he said. I know don't worry about it, he can do whatever but I'll show him why I'm the alpha, prepare for tonight, Now! "Keep your anger in check tonight, please Jimin, you know you are being watched, any mistake the clans will question your authority and let the Aurimary Clan know, be careful", he looked at me with dead shot serious eyes. I know Jungkook, I appreciate you being there, even after all we have been through you're still here." I am sorry too for all I did, especially letting Hajimin use me, I thought I would get power, I owe Y/n an apology for everything especially raping her, I didn't know what came over me but it can't excuse my actions and I will understand if she never forgives me", he looked down lost in thought. It's in the past, though you do it again, I'll kill you myself and that's final. Now, let's get ready for tonight.

Y/n P.o.v

Miyeon my baby why are you screaming and calling me like this, is everything okay? "Mommy can I ask you something?" he sat on top of me cupping both my cheeks with his tiny hands. Yes honey, what's the matter? "Do you love me?" he asked. Yes my baby, why are you asking? "Would you do anything for me if I asked you?" he asked again. Anything, tell me why are you asking all this? You are starting to worry me. " Please mommy, love my daddy back, so that we can be a family", he said looking down, his words left my mouth empty, cold as snow, like a knife cutting through my heart. I can't baby, he doesn't want that, I waited for him for a long time but he never came. "No, mommy he's hiding something from you", he said. How do you know this, my baby? "When I feed off him, I feel something, a link so deep", he looked down. What? Why didn't you tell me this huh? "I'm scared of what he can do if he turns bad, I've seen him, mommy, his eyes turn blue, he just needs me and you to help him control his anger, without us he might die", he looked at me with pitiful eyes. I just can't my baby, he made his choice, and so will I, I've chosen to move on, I'm so sorry baby. "Can you at least think about it mommy for my sake, please", he asked. Okay Miyeon, mommy will think about it, promise you'll behave yourself tonight in return. "Okay mommy, I promise, but be careful tonight, I'm feeling bad vibes", he said. Look at my baby talking like any adult, okay we will be careful, let me get ready, I put on a black and red mid-length dress that shaped all my curves and a dash of makeup and I looked like I belonged with a vampire damn. Tae why are you looking at me like that? "Wow, just wow, you look so hot and beautiful my Rose. I blushed, thank you, you look breathtaking yourself, I took a look at him from his hair to his shoes, losing words, he was handsome in his deep black tux and a dark red shirt, and he looked so hot. " Girl stop looking at me like that, you are the one breath-taking, tonight all eyes will be on you", he placed a kiss on my lips and neck. Come on Tae, let's go we already getting late and if we start this we won't stop, you blush. "Fine, fine, let's go, and we made our way. We got there and saw a lot of people but the moment Tae wrapped his hands around my waist all eyes were fixed on us. "Told you, you looking smocking hot", he grinned. Thank you, geez you making me blush hard today. "Cause you my lady and you deserve it duh, let's go dance, the whole pack must see you, I like showing off hahaha", he smirked. That I know you do, I let him lead me to the dance room, and he grabbed me by my waist not allowing any space between us, we looked at each other like we were the only ones in that very room. "You so beautiful Y/n", he whispered. I smiled, no I don't know that. "Ohh you are my rose", he leaned close, inches from kissing you. Tae.... . "What?" he asked. No words came out, he cupped my face, placing a kiss on my lips, and he deepened it, kissing me passionately. He locked his tongue with mine, and we kissed for about 5 minutes but something made us stop. I know it was him, his presence was always intoxicating to me, I could feel he was near me which made me fear upon thinking about Miyeon's words earlier. He's here, and you knew he would see this, why would you do this Tae huh?" You are my date Y/n, if he doesn't like it, he can suck it up", he said. Tae, we will discuss this when we get home, let's try and enjoy the rest of the evening. "Fine, your wish is my command, my lady.

Jimin P.o.v

I sighed. I sighed again. "Don't do anything, remember you're being watched tonight, "Jungkook said bringing me to my senses. I know Taehyung is doing this on purpose, he wants me to get angry, but not tonight not when I'm alpha, he has no idea what I'm capable of. I pushed myself and passed them not saying a word and not showing any emotion but deep down it hurt so much especially the way he held and kissed her, damn fuck my pathetic life. Jungkook, I want to get some air and clear my mind, I will be back, make sure you deal with those snitches. "Okay, but don't forget, no anger Jimin", he said. I know, stop reminding me, or I'll get pissed and take it out on you. " I'm doing it for you but fine, go get some air and come back and enjoy yourself, it's a good event and I prepared a surprise for you", he smirked. Geez fine, I left and went deep into a hidden place only I knew and no one could sense or read my thoughts, where it was a Zen place of no connection to my pack and Y/n especially.

Y/n P.o.v

Hey Tae, can I go outside, I need some air from all these vampires, they all looking and licking their lips, and it's making me feel uncomfortable. "Hahahaha don't worry, they wouldn't dare touch you, they know what I will do to them, go and come back, let me mingle for now", he kissed me and I left. I kept strolling not knowing where I was going, till I reached a peaceful place, all I could sense was his presence which kept pulling me closer to him. Seeing him made me quiver. "What are you doing here? He looked up at me. I got lost, I was taking a walk, then it became dark, I'm sorry for disturbing you. "You not disturbing me, how is Miyeon doing?" he asked. He's okay, just eager to see you again. "Ohh I will, I'm also looking forward to seeing him", he said. Can I ask you something Jimin? "It depends on whether I have an answer for it", he replied coldly. What changed? "I'm not sure I follow, what changed where?" he looked down. You know between me and you, the love we shared, what went wrong? Was it me? Was I not good enough for you? Or maybe I was not good enough for an alpha. "No Y/n, it's not that, it's a reason I can't give you", he looked at me why? "Anyway, why does it matter, you moved on with Tae, does it make a difference", he looked deep into my soul. It matters to me because.... Before I could finish that he pulled me making me sit on his lap. Why do you make things hard? I can feel this between us, the fire we create, every feeling we have is real but you make things hard for us......He smashed his lips with mine not allowing me space to move or react.

Chapter 24

" I'm sorry", he said. For what? "For kissing you, I couldn't stop myself, I................" he grew silent. "It won't happen again", he looked down. Why are you sorry Jimin huh? Didn't that mean anything to you? He grew silent........." Y/n go, someone is coming", he stood ghastly looking worried. Are you sure or it's an excuse to avoid answering me? "I am dead serious right now, go straight that way, you'll go to the party, ask Tae to take you straight home, don't look suspicious, there's trouble, "he said looking angry. You know I can stay with you if you need me. "Just go Y/n, please go", he said. I left in the direction he told me to go.

Jimin P.o.v

What do you want huh? "I want to challenge you to be alpha, you damn too weak for it", the clanless vampire spoke loudly and angrily. What makes you think you are stronger than me? " well that's cause you are smitten over that bimbo who doesn't even love you, we all know what happened between that bitch of a girl and you", he spoke not caring. Anger overtook me but Jung kook's words remained imprinted in my mind, what if this was a test, if I respond to him I would just be killed by the Aurimary clan and no one would even notice? Get out of here, there are ways to challenge an alpha, if you do this I will kill you in front of the whole clan. "Hahahaha, that's if you can", he laughed and attacked stabbing me with a knife that was dipped in, Chinese sense, a weakness to all vampires. No, you can't do this, the incense was weakening me quickly. "This is just the beginning, I will be alpha, I'm stronger than you", he left in a hurry.

Y/n P.o.v

"Hey Y/n, where have you been?" he hugged me from behind. Let's go home Tae. "What's wrong? You look so scared and shaken up", he asked looking worried. Please can we go now, I have to check on Miyeon, please Tae, something is not right, and I can feel it. He didn't respond just pulled me by the right hand and lead me out, making our way home, we were able to find Miyeon sleeping. My baby is so peaceful, I'm guessing his nanny put him to sleep now." Mam, I'll be off now, he was no bother today, he spent the whole day quietly like he was thinking about something, may I take my leave? she asked. Okay, thank you so much for everything, I will talk to him when he wakes up, for now, you may leave, thank you for everything, she nodded and left. "Y/n, talk to me, you just took a walk and you came back scared, what the hell happened?" he asked. I saw Jimin, but he was in trouble, he asked me to get you and we leave because they were after me or Miyeon, I just got scared and I left, for now, let's get some rest, we will figure it out later. He kissed my lips softly and led me to bed. "Thank you for tonight and for going with me", he said. You don't need to thank me, I feel we both needed this.

Jimin P.o.v

"What the hell happened to you, you look finished and pale", he asked as he helped me. I ......neee...d... b, I coughed blood, I need blood....I coughed again. "But you know for this type of attack only Y/n can save you", he said. No, don't bring her into this Jungkook, please. "I can't watch you like this", he looked at me pitifully. I'll be fine, don't worry about me, just get me a lot of blood, it must not be Y/n's remember what it does to me." Let me get you blood, rest now", he said as he left running.

Y/n P.o.v

Miyeon came running again, waking me up from sleep. What's wrong baby? "I need to see daddy now," he said. What do you mean my baby huh? He started crying, "Something is wrong mommy, I can feel his pain, it's killing him", he sniffled his tears. I saw him tonight baby and to me, he seemed fine." No mommy, please", he cried again. Okay, baby stop crying please, let's go, if it will make you feel better. "Thank you, mommy, he said as he stopped crying. I know he's okay my baby so don't worry okay, I put a coat on him as the weather was very chilly at night, and we made our way to Jimin's place, my heart was racing so fast. "What are you doing here Y/n? You are not welcome here", Jungkook said. I know but I need to have a word with Jimin, it's important as you can see I came so late with his son. "I'm sorry but he made it clear that he doesn't want to see you, alpha's orders", he smirked. I have no intention of seeing him but his son was crying all night wanting to see him, get out of my way Jungkook, or I will hurt you, remember how strong I am. "Hahaha I would like to see you try", he smirked. I gathered all my strength and pushed him hard making him fall, we made our way to Jimin's room." Ohh I'm fucked, coughing blood again, no blood is working, I feel like shit", Jimin cried out in pain. "Daddy, daddy, I knew something was wrong, I felt it", Miyeon rushed to his father. "Come on my son, what are you doing here, so late, I hate you seeing me like this", he said looking so much in pain." Daddy I had to, I feel your pain remember", he started crying." Don't cry Miyeon, I'm okay you see", he coughed a lot of blood. Jimin let me help you, it pained me seeing him like that." Y/n you can help me by taking him home, I don't want him to see me like this, I will be fine", he said. No Jimin, you know I can't leave you like this, he won't sleep much, and he's just like you." And how am I", he asked. Stubborn as hell but not today, you'll be doing it for your son, not me. "Please daddy, listen to mommy or you'll die, I don't want you to leave me before you train me to be like you, please daddy," he said. "Are you sure about this Y/n?" he asked. Yes, I am sure, 100% sure, I brought myself closer to him as he took my blood, and it strengthened him, making him stop. "Thank you both of you", he said and passed out. Jimin, Jimin, wake up, please." What's wrong with daddy and mommy? He asked looking at me with sorrowful eyes. I'm not sure, as panic arose in me. "Both of you need to leave now because we know how he will be when he wakes up and he wouldn't want to hurt you." Jungkook said. Okay, let's go, baby, Jungkook please keep us updated when he wakes up, and I do apologize for pushing you. "Don't mention it, I will update you don't worry, I am sorry for everything too", he looked at me. It's okay, I kinda forgave you long back I figured it wasn't you doing all that and my suspicion turned out to be true. We are leaving now, please don't forget to update us, we left and made our way home. "Where the hell have you been Y/n, I've been worried sick", Tae asked as soon as I put Miyeon to bed. Miyeon wanted to see Jimin, he was crying endlessly. "And why the hell was that?" he asked looking angry. He was hurt very bad, I do apologize for not telling you Tae, please forgive me, as I saw his eyes turning dark." You couldn't tell me that, why did you lie to me Y/n, am I a fool in your eyes?" he asked. No, you are not a fool Tae, it's not what you think. "What do I think exactly huh?" he asked. That I didn't mean every word I said to you, but I did every word of it. I only went cause of Miyeon and nothing else. You know I hate seeing him cry, please, believe me, I wouldn't lie to you, and I hate fighting like this with you, please Tae. He stood there silently for a few seconds and the only thing I felt was a sharp stinging pain on my left cheek as I just notice he slapped me.

Chapter 25

I'm sorry Tae but why did you slap me huh? "Cause I hate it when you say that you want to be with me but you still have strong feelings for Jimin", he looks at me. No Tae, I pull him and kiss him. Stop it Tae, stop being insecure, I'm here ain't I? If I wanted Jimin, I would have left. Yes, I do love him, and he knows that but everything ended between us the only tie we have is Miyeon. I will stop him from being there for my son. I want to be with you, I want to be happy and you make me happy. I hate it when you fight with me, especially over or about him, and I don't want to talk about him. I pull him closer to me, our lips almost touching. "I'm sorry Y/n for slapping you, and acting like a jealous boyfriend", he said looking deep into my eyes. But you are mine Tae, and you have every right to be, he cups my chin and kisses me deeply not letting me go, no space was between us. "I want you Y/n, only if you allow me, you know I will never let you do anything you are not comfortable with", he breathed in my ear as he whispered. Well, I want you as I've never wanted anyone, I pull him hard and make him smile. "Easy tigress, I know you're strong but this is just hot", he smirked. Tae stop talking and work boy right now before I hurt you. "Let's see what you can do princess", he smirked again. He pulled me by the waist, kissing me, our tongues locked together, as he made me sit on top of him. Tae............passion rose between us. "What?" he asked. You're so handsome, he unzipped my dress. "You the beautiful one", as he caressed my body, looking at my bare chest, we were both turned on.

Tae...... I kissed as naked as I was, deepening the kiss, readying myself for what he was about to do to me. He made love to me like a hungry beast devouring its prey slowly, never, not once taking his eyes off me.

Jimin P.o.v

The good and evil in me are colliding, and I can't turn the voices off, it's what causes me to lose control. "This is the last time you transform, the next time either you die or go bad", the good side spoke. I would rather die, than watch Tae take everything I love, yet I can't even do anything about it because it looks like Y/n has made her choice. "Shut up both of you, yes, yes, I'm back to knock some sense into your thick empty skull", my evil side spoke with such confidence. Get thee behind me, I have no use of you, I don't want to be bad or hurt the ones I love, my son is all that matters. "Then you have to live for him", the good side spoke. They already had sex Jimin, what if she gets pregnant? Will you live with that huh, the way he touches her, the way he eats her hahaha", the evil side spoke. Stop it, the thought of it pained me so much. " stop it yourself Jimin, show her you love her, she's doing this because she feels you not man enough to stand up to your brother, you always fuck and leave her but Tae stays and takes good care of both of them", the good side spoke again. Then it means I am not alpha material if I can't do that, but I have to think about my son, he's all I have besides those two idiots I call brothers. " Then all I can tell you is Man up, she is yours, she was yours first and will always be, you broke her virginity Jimin, you shared the blood with her that made you one, no matter how many men she sleeps with, she will never have that with anyone else", the good side spoke again. How do I even man up when she already made her choice, huh, and I can't change that or force her to leave tae and follow me so that I hurt her all over again? " Then you don't deserve to be an alpha, you know the laws, they will take your son if you don't have a wife when he turns the required age, then I suggest you fight with all that you have left in that human heart of yours", the good side spoke as he left. I am screwed now, fuck this, how will I even man up to

Y/n, making her sleep with us both is not the option I want, she is not some toy to be tossed around like she has no value.

Y/n P.o.v

Tae, I'm going to the mall, I need to get this baby bear of mine clothes, and he's growing so quickly. "Want me to come with you?" he smirked. No please, I blushed, failing to look at him, Who gonna watch Miyeon? "Do you regret yesterday?" he smirked. No, should I? "No, was just asking, 'cause you were amazing Y/n", he pulls me and kisses me not letting go, at this rate my lips will be even more swollen than they are. I'm going, 'cause if we start this we won't stop, he smirks as I leave watching me from behind, it's like I could tell his eyes were checking me up from top to bottom. I make my way to the mall, but his presence was there, it was always that dark and dangerous scent that turned me on without even seeing him. How could he have such strong power over me but this time something was different. Is it me or what? He passed me not looking at me as if he didn't know me. Has he truly forgotten me, I fail to believe that, I finish up buying stuff and take a walk by silent creek park. "Hi Luna, did I scare you?" he looked at me standing in front of me. No, it's just........I failed to say anything. "Just what?" he asked. You just acted like you didn't know me when I saw you at the mall. "Do I know this Y/n? He came closer to me. What do you mean? "She would not do this to me if she claimed she loved me", he drew closer till we were almost kissing. Jimin I .... "Shhhh don't explain it", he looked deep into my should making my heart beat so fast, he kissed me, deepening it, and he let go as I kissed him back following the rhythm he was going at. "You should know who you want Y/n, I want an honest answer, him or the father of your child", he smirked. But I ..... "Shhhh, I told you, no explanations, think about it", he leaves. What do I do now? Tears fell. Jimin is confusing me, he's different, and like the first, we met. He took over me like how I was weak for him today. How could I just kiss him and not fight back, if he loves me then he has a weird way of showing it. What about Tae? He's been there for me, taking care of both me and my son. We just had amazing sex, sex with a half-breed is awesome but with alpha, it's even hotter. I'm so confused, but as I walk something caught my eye. "I wanted to see if you had the power Hajimin spoke about", she spoke. Who are you? "I'm the dark Siren, feared among man, and the little boy you gave birth to is causing havoc, how dare you keep him", the siren spoke with a thunderous voice. What do you mean, there's nothing wrong with my son. "You foolish girl, he holds the power of the guardian vampire and the power of the moon, mix those two, he'll take out a lot of monsters including us", she spoke looking worried. No, he won't, because he has a human heart. She slaps me. "Shut up, stupid girl, you don't know that, or maybe you should ask the boy's father, what happens when he transforms for the last time", she spoke laughing. Since you said you are of the siren sirens, why are you telling me all of this? " Cause I'm scared, we all are, I'm the last of my kind, and we have lived for centuries, and we have never seen anything like this, a lot of people want him dead", she said. He is my son and I will protect him. " Only his father can, with their power combined they can shun it light and save us all from the darkness but talk to him because something is coming his way, till we meet again", she whirls away in the windy weather that just appeared from nowhere. Wooooooow, just Wooooooow can my day confuse me even more? It's like I can never rest damn my life. I manage to reach home still shocked by this encounter. "Hey baby, how was the mall? Did you get everything you needed?" Tae asked looking at me. Yes, I did, and you guys stay okay? "Yes, Miyeon and I were playing till he fell asleep", he said right before we were disturbed by a knock that startled me. "I'll get it", he said. "Jimin, what the hell are you doing here? What's wrong? As he noticed blood all over Jimin, he passed out before he could answer anything.

Chapter 26

❝ He's still not waking up, I've given him a lot of blood but he's still not waking up", Tae looked at Jimin worried. Should I try my blood? "Let me take Miyeon out of here, you know how he is when he wakes up, but it will save him, that's the only shot we have to take", he looks at me. Okay, you guys also be safe, we don't know who did this, and they might still be outside or nearby. "Okay Y/n, be safe", he kissed me and left. I drew some blood from my arm to feed Jimin but before I could he weakly pushed me away. "No not your blood", he said. No Jimin, it's the only thing that can save you. "No Y/n, it will kill me", he moves away from me fighting the urge to drink my blood. No blood is working Jimin, you know mine can heal you. "I SAID NO! Leave me alone, I'll be fine". He looked so much in pain. I'm sorry I was only trying to help, I left not looking back. "What happened? Why are you looking gloomy huh? HE refused. "Why? But he knows it can heal him", Tae looked shocked upon hearing that. I've never seen him so angry, I decided to let him be, where is my baby? "He went to play", He said. Okay, I want to wash this, I'll be back, I make my way to the washroom lost in thought, wondering what was going in Jimin's mind.

Jimin P.o.v

I hate doing this to her but if I transform either I die or become bad for eternity and I don't want either. "Daddy, can I sit with you?" Miyeon said looking at me with those beautiful puppy-like eyes. Yeah sure, what are you doing here? Your mom won't be pleased. "I came to see you, why didn't you tell mommy what would happen if you took her blood? He looked at me. Because of my son, she worries a lot, and I don't want her to think I'm lying. "So what will you do daddy, you don't look so good, wanna try my blood?" he asked looking excited. What are you asking my son, I can't you too young? "Exactly, meaning it won't harm you like mom, I'm strong daddy, after all, I am your son", he smiled. Your mom would never allow you to do this, my son. "So we don't tell her then, daddy I don't want you to die, and you also have to be open to mommy, please", he begged me. Okay, thank you so much, my baby, for doing this, I manage to take his blood but with a few drops my bones healed making me even stronger than I was." See, I'm okay and you okay", he smiled happily. All I could do is hug him. You are my light, and I will fight for you, and will always protect you. " what happened to you, you look fine, and you little man, I've been looking for you everywhere, Y/n walked in like a queen she is. " I came to see daddy, and found him looking much better, I'm now happy mommy", Miyeon laughed while looking at me. "Okay baby, go and play with uncle Tae, I want to have a word with your dad", she said looking at me as Miyeon disappeared from my sight

Y/n P.o.v

How the hell did you get better, I thought only my blood could heal a guardian vampire. "I wasn't hurt like before, I just needed to rest and recuperate," he said. Who hurt you? "That's not for you to know, just know someone wanted to hurt my son and I fought them and they stabbed me with some incense", he said looking annoyed. And that is not for me huh? He pulled me making me sit on him, "Nope it's not for you to know, imma want my answer, that's more important Luna", and he smirked. What answer? "You didn't get me the first time, ohh Luna, you should listen", he kissed me passionately never letting go of my waist, and he smirked. Jimin I............. "I'm going, I need to have a word with Tae", he smirked again. Okay, I just froze there, it's like my limbs were frozen everywhere.

Jimin P.o.v

"Jimin, who keeps attacking you?" he asked looking at me. Someone after my son, please don't leave them alone. Make sure the pack watches them, this might be the last time seeing you, anything happens, please take care of my son. Don't let anything hurt both of them, I'm counting on you Tae, to help me on this. "You have to take care of your son, what do you mean anything?" he asked looking worried. Tae, you are my family, regards all that's happened, we share the same blood. Jungkook will tell you what to do if I don't come back in a week, I gather myself and hug him. Take care of yourself and my family, I love you brother, and I just left not looking back.

Y/n P.o.v

Little man, come here and tell mommy what you and your father are plotting. "Nothing mommy", he smiled. So where did you get these bite marks? "Nowhere mommy", he said looking down. Tell me the truth NOW! "I told daddy to take my blood", he smiled and looked down. And you did, he could have killed you, baby. "No, you could have killed him", he said looking upset. What are you talking about baby huh? "If he took your blood he would have died or turned evil but mine made him strong", he smiled. You are so grown up, I can't even catch up with you and your father. Thank you, my son, for being the best son ever. " Hey Y/n, I'm going out, I'll be back soon, the pack will be around to look after you and to make sure you are well-taken care of", Tae looked at me. Okay, Hunny, be safe, he kissed me as he made his way out.

Tae P.o.v

"What brings you here? The clanless vampire spoke looking at me. I need a favor. "Give me a reason as to why I should trust you?" he asked looking at me. It's not your business, first answer me, why do you want to be alpha? " Because that idiot Jimin chooses that bitch over his clan, he doesn't care about us all, he just uses us all as if we don't matter", he said still looking me dead in the eyes. What if you lose then what?

Cause you are aware he's the strongest of all living and dead vampires. "Well I know what to do to be alpha, no matter what it takes, he won't see this coming, he spoke angrily looking at me. Hmmm, interesting. "So now, are you here to question me or to ask me something?" he asked. Make sure this stays between us because if they find out I asked you, I'll kill you myself. "You kill me hahahahahaha, you just a boy", he laughed again. Then you don't know anything about me, because where I come from you should be afraid of me. Me afraid? Never will that happen, now tell me what is it you want?" he smirked. When you battle Jimin to be alpha, I want you to do something for me. "What is it you desire?" he asked. Make sure you kill him permanently.

Chapter 27

Jimin P.o.v

I need your help. "Why?" they asked. Because they will try to cheat and kill me, my brother has betrayed me. "We are aware, but you don't need our help", they said. What do you mean? "You already have the power, show what it means to be a guardian vampire, you were chosen among us to look over every vampire, you knew falling in love with her would cost you but now that you have a seedling, his power is, even more, stronger than yours and you will have to take him to the alpha ceremony when he comes of age", they said. How do I do that? "You will have to intake both mother and son's blood", they said. I don't understand. "Use your head Alpha, mix their blood then nothing can harm you, even if they try, you'll be the most power fullest guardian", he said. "But let me warn you, don't be foolish Jimin, we chose you as Aurimary for a reason, don't make us end you", the other member spoke. I know. "Now leave and pay heed of our words", they spoke together at once. I have heard you, but if it fails then what? "Have we ever been wrong so far?" they questioned me. No. "THEN LEAVE!!!!!!

Y/n P.o.v

"Mommy, I'm not feeling too good", he cries. What's wrong baby? "No mommy, I must sleep, wake me up when daddy comes, he'll know what to do", he sleeps. What the hell is this now? How on earth will I find Jimin? What the hell Miyeon? "Mam, are you going somewhere?"

Miyeon's nanny asks. Yes, if Tae comes, tell him I'm searching for Jimin, something is wrong with Miyeon. "Okay mam, Will do so", she smiles. Also, lock the doors and don't open them for anyone unless it's me, Jimin, or Tae, only. "I understand mam", I wave goodbye and leave. Why do I have to go through this for my son? Let me go check at the place we first met, the magical day that was, I make my way there and find him lost in thought. Hie Jimin. "Hi Luna, why are you here?" he asked not looking at me. Miyeon is asking for you. "Is he okay?" he stood. He said you will know what to do. "Okay, let's go, after we deal with him, Me and you need to talk", he said looking pale. We made our way home, but we didn't speak or look at each other.

Jimin P.o.v

Leave us Y/n, will call you when I figure out what is wrong. She doesn't protest or anything. Miyeon, wake up my son, daddy is here. "Daddy I was scared", he hugs me early. Why? "You know daddy, uncle Tae wants you dead," he snuffles. How do you know that huh? "I see what you see, remember daddy", he looks at me. Don't worry or be scared, I need your and mommy's blood to live okay, I'll draw yours first then mommy's blood. "Okay daddy, I'll be okay", he smiles as I draw his blood. You are my brave soldier, I love you, my son, never forget that. "I love you too daddy", he smiles. Go and play with aunty while I talk to mommy. "Okay daddy, thank you", he leaves.

Y/n P.o.v

What was wrong with him Jimin, what are you two hiding? "Close the door, matter of fact lock it, and we talk", he smirks. Is everything okay? "Does it look okay?" he asked. No. I closed the door and locked it. "Come here", he made me sit on top of him. Jimin .... What are .....? Before I could finish speaking he smashed his lips on mine, biting them and making them swell. "You know what's mine, will always be mine, you're my soulmate after all Y/n", he smirked. Then why did you leave me for three full years huh? "Because I couldn't be with you till my son was old enough", he said not taking his eyes away from mine. Was it so hard for you to tell me?" It's not about this Y/n, it's about this Luna, how much I want you right here right now, and he kissed me again. J....I moan his name but he smirked at the way I responded to his touch. "You so fuckin adorable Y/n, my Luna", he kisses my neck. "So this is wassup, I want you here and right now, and there is no stopping me once I start if you don't want to leave", he smirked. I don't want to leave, I want you Jimin. He grabs me by the waist, damn my hormones to this incredible vampire. He undressed me. "You such a goddess", he embraced my breasts, heavy breathing on me, making my nipples harden while he bit me gently. That made me moan damn Jimin, no vampire has ever made me feel like this. He rhythmically moved his hand, the same as how my heart was beating. Pressing his soft fingers on my thighs, he spread my legs open while kissing them. "Look at you dripping for me", he kissed me. J......Jimin..........I. " Shh, Luna, let your body do the talking", he penetrated deep in me moving slow and fast in a way that made me release an orgasm that shook, he made an animal sound as reached his climate realizing his semen deep in me making me drip." F.....fuck Luna, what you doing to me, why do you have to be this sweet", he said as we controlled our breathing. No words were coming from me, no man has ever made love to me the way you do Jimin. "I need your blood Y/n", he said. What? I thought you said it will kill you." Imma go bad Y/n in case this is my last time, that is why I wanted to make love to you and make you keep me inside your heart and memories, I love you get that Y/n, I'M FUCKING IN LOVE WITH YOU", he said. Then don't go bad, please. "You rather I die?" he looked at me. No, we figure it out together. "No Y/n, you with Tae", he looked at me. I cannot lose you Jimin, I love you. "Well Tae also wants me to die, so he can have you all to himself", he looked down. What do you mean? He's your brother. " He was not until he made an option to get me killed, it's better I go bad than die right?", he kisses me as he takes my blood mixing it with Miyeon's but it's like he was avoiding me seeing that. Jimin doesn't leave me, please. "No Y/n, I'm doing this for you and my son, you should ask Tae what he did to Rose if you don't believe what I just told you", he pull me in for a hug. " Kiss Miyeon for me, and tell him I love him, I love you no matter what happens tonight, you'll always be mine Y/n remember that I fucking love you Y/n keep that in mind, I love you", he leaves not looking back. What the hell am I supposed to do with all this? How could he make love to me like this and leave me, tears fell even though I don't understand what is going on with Jimin, all I could feel is he was leaving me for good.

Chapter 28

Y/n P.o.v

"Y/n why are you looking so lost, I've been calling out to you", Tae looked at me. It's nothing, I'm just tired Miyeon wasn't feeling well. "What's wrong?" He wanted to see Jimin. "Why?" How should I know, he wanted his father, hey. "Okay, where are you going dressed like this?" he kissed me. I want to see Lisa, I want to fix everything with those guys, especially uncle Kai, I miss them so much. "Okay hurry back, I have a surprise for you", he smiles at me. Okay, I'll be back, I'm going with Miyeon, and I want to introduce him to his aunty. "Okay baby, go or I won't let you go," he placed a kiss on my lips and I managed to leave.

"Mommy do you love daddy?" Miyeon looked at me. Why are you asking me baby huh? "Yes or no?" he asked. Yes, I do. "Why are we not staying together as a family?" he asked again. Baby not now, I'll explain everything later, behave okay, we are meeting people. "Sorry mommy", he goes silent. Hey Lisa, sorry we are a bit late, she hurriedly hugs Miyeon, ignoring me. "Hello little one, what's your name? She smiles at him. "I'm Miyeon", he said shyly. "Aren't you so adorable, I'm your aunty Lisa, nice to meet you", she smiles at him. Am I invisible? "Come here", she hugs me as if she was seeing a huge cuddly teddy bear. "Why do you look so pale and full of scars huh?" she observes me. It's nothing, don't worry about it. "We are family, and I hate how you left, how upset you were", she looks at me. I know me too, I missed this, and I missed you. "Me too Y/n, you the only best friend I have", uncle appears. Hi, uncle I wanted to..... He hugs me before I could finish what I was saying. "I'm so sorry Y/n", he apologizes. No uncle, I'm sorry for everything and for the way I left, it was selfish of me. "It's okay, I'm glad you came", he smiles. I want you to meet your nephew, this is Miyeon, he quickly hugs him not letting go. "He's so adorable", he smiles again. "Hi uncle, mommy has told me so much about you", he smiles. "Good things I hope", he smirks. "Y/n, you have to talk to Rose, she's coming here now", he looks at me. But uncle last time, she said I'm not her sister. "I believe you have to talk", he pleads. "We do Y/n", she arrives, and they leave with Miyeon, to give you privacy. What do you want huh? You disowned me remember? "Uncle explained everything, I'm sorry Y/n", she falls to her knees crying. No Rose, don't cry, I know losing mom hasn't been easy but we need each other. I need you, you are practically my mother. "I'm sorry Y/n, what can I do to make you forgive me?" She looks at me with apologetic eyes. Tell me what Taehyung did. "Y/n I ...., tears fall as she speaks, I was his girlfriend till he hurt me", she cried. I couldn't even find words like what the hell, how did he hurt you huh?

Time Remanence

Rose P.o.v

Tae Tae, do you love me? "More than my whole existence", he smiles. Then don't leave me. "You know I won't, I love you", he kisses my hand which made me feel like I was a queen. I know you do. "I want you", he smirked. I told you Tae Tae, I'm just not ready for it. "Who said I was asking, but first I need your blood", he draws my blood. Tae what's come over you huh? "What I should have done, you are so sweet, your scent is like a drug to me, it's too addictive", he smirked again. Taehyung, no please, what's wrong with you, tears flooded my eyes. "Stop fake crying, it's not getting you outta here, now strip for me, I want you to obey me, if you don't who knows what I will do", he laughed. No please, I tried to leave but he blocked my path and his strength was too much. "Don't try that Rose, my Rose, no one will ever touch you", he tore my dress leaving me with only underwear. Tears continued to flow, as I begged him to stop. "Why? When you are this attractive, he pushes me on the bed. Now open your legs, don't fight me Rose", he smirked as he pinned my hands down. No please, don't hurt me, I'll leave you and will never see you, I won't tell anyone who or what you are. "Do I look like I care? He penetrated me, raping me. You are so fucking adorable, he pleasures himself while hurting me. We are done Rose, If you ever tell anyone this, I'll kill that little sister of yours and drink her blood in front of you", he smirked and left leaving me bloody and dirty.

Y/n P.o.v

Ohh my God, he rapped you? Why didn't you tell me or say anything Rose? "What exactly? That I was broken by a man I was deep in love with", she looks at me. I'm sorry, tears emitted from my eyes, I'm sorry, that very same Tae is with me now, and if I had known I would have never agreed. "I know", she looks at me. How do you know? " I saw you with him, and for the first time you were so happy, why would I take that away from you huh?", she hugged me not letting go. I need a favor first, but come and meet your son Miyeon. . "You think he'll like me? Miyeon runs and hugs her. "Hie mommy, you are my mommy too, I know because mommy is always talking about you", he smiles at her. "Nice to meet you too little one, Y/n what's the favor you wanted?" she looks at me. I want you to face Tae, there's something I want to find out. "Y/n but....." she goes silent. No buts, time to face him, I want to find out something and it might just save both my and Miyeon's life. "I'll do it for you, let's go", she hugs me again.

Jimin P.o.v

I take the blood again, but a huge serge-like feeling flows all over me. What is happening to me? Stronger currents overpowered me as my eyes turned black and blue. I feel so strong, this strength is just so great. I neee to feed as hunger overtook me.

Y/n P.o.v

"Y/n I ....." she looks at me with nervous eyes. Don't worry I am with you, he won't do anything to you. "Are you sure? She looks at me. He knows what I can do. "And what is that? And promise you won't leave me", she asks. You'll see don't worry, I promise, you won't be alone, let's get Miyeon safe first, we drop him off at his nanny's place. "I love you mommy", he smiles at me. I love you too, I'll come to get you, behave yourself. We leave and make our way home. Tae, I, I notice him bleeding, what happened? "What the hell is she doing here?" he looks at Rose. I'll tell you but first answer me damn it. "I......he passes out bleeding profusely. Taehyung, wake up, what happened? He wakes up in so much pain. "Y/n, I'm so sorry, for everything I did. It was not me, I was under the influence of, and he coughs, the siren". What? What do you mean? " It's not the first time she used me like this, the first time was with Rose either Rose dies or I lost her, all they wanted was her blood", he looks down. Jimin tried to end the Siren but she hid and didn't stop, till yesterday she visited me.

Time Reminisce

Tae P.o.v

What are you doing here? "To offer you a deal", she laughs. I want nothing to do with you, leave me, please. "Don't you want Y/n to be yours forever without Jimin", she asks looking serious. I love her but I would never force her on me, it's her choice. "You such a fool, but anyway you kinda don't have a choice", she laughs. Says who huh? "Hahaha me you idiot", she blows some dust-like powder onto my eyes. What have you done to me? "Akerus", she chanted. "You are now spellbound to me, now you do as I say, or I will end you", she chants again. Yes, I know. "End Jimin, am I clear?" she asked. Yes crystal clear.

Y/n P.o.v

"So when Jimin mixed you and Miyeon's blood, a wave hit all of us alerting us of our Alpha's great power, she came and attacked me, then she said she is not done with me", he winces in pain. Wait go back, you said Jimin did what? "He mixed you and Miyeon's blood", he looked at me puzzled. I can't believe him, why did he lie to me then? " Most probably cause he thinks, I want him dead, we have to find him Y/n, you are the only one who can bring him back and down, only you", he looks at me. "Taehyung, what the hell?" she asks. "I'm so sorry Rose", he knelt in tears. "Why didn't you tell me, when her spell faded, all this time I thought you were a monster", she kneels next to him. "I'm sorry for taking your blood, raping you, abusing your love, I'm truly sorry, after all, we went through, I don't deserve your forgiveness", he looks at her. "It's okay, it was not you, at least now I know the truth", she smiles at him." Y/n, I'm sorry", he looks at me. For what? "For not telling you about Rose, I really should have told you in the beginning before we slept together and created all these wonderful memories together", he smiles at me. It's okay Tae, I kinda forgave you long back, I knew but just needed to get all facts right. We are disturbed by a knock. "Let me check first, you girls be safe", he goes and opens the door. "What are you doing here?" he looks at Jungkook. "We need Miyeon, it's important", he looks at Tae. Why the hell do you need my son? "He knows what to do", he looked me dead serious in the eyes. What are you talking about, you look really scared. "Where is he Y/n?" he asked again. First, tell me what's going on huh? "It's Jimin", he looks down. What about him? "He's killing again", he looks down scared. "That's not good, we need to go Y/n", Tae suggests. Will you tell me what's wrong? "Yes, but we have to go if you still want him alive", he looks at me. "He won the alpha title, but he just became grand alpha by killing his opponent", he responded. "No, no, no that's very bad, let's get Miyeon, Y/n did you leave him with his nanny?" he asked. Yes, I did, let's go, Rose, I'll see you later right? "Yes, I have some business to take care of", she hugs me. Thank you for everything today but please don't tell anyone about this. "Don't worry Y/n, your secret is safe with me, we sisters remember, I love you and be safe, now go", she hugs me again and we leave. We find Miyeon crying. What's wrong baby huh, why are you crying? "It's daddy, we have to stop him before he kills himself", he cries. How do you know that huh? "Because I see what he sees remember", his eyes turn golden yellow leaving me out of words. "I wanted to tell you but you didn't listen to daddy, now he might die", he looks at me sniffling tears. He won't die, my baby, we will find a way to save him. "He doesn't want to be saved", he cries. "He means Jimin wants to end his life in front of the Aurimary clan, if he surrenders to them they take his power, and are killed in front of all clans, he once almost did it, and it broke him. I might be bad, but he's my brother and I will do anything for him, even though I've hurt him so much, I want him alive, who will I fight huh?" he looks at me. "You should have thought about that before having his girl", Jungkook looks at him angrily. "He knew I liked her way before this, I did what any guy would do, became a man, and raised his son, where was he? Ohh right going through Trans, so spare me the talk Jungkook, even so, you rapped her", he looks at Jungkook angrily. Guy's geez, I'm right here you know. "I'm sorry Y/n, it's just that he gets on my nerves, but now let's find Jimin.

Jimin P.o.v

I don't want this power, it has made me do things I didn't want to do, and I killed innocent people today. All because I could not control it. Then how am I a dad huh, Miyeon deserves Tae? He's a better man than I am, he looks after them so well, I deserve death, I'm a monster, forgive me, son, I love you, you see my love for you. Grow up and be a brave soldier take care of mommy, and always be a good boy. Daddy loves you a lot keep that in mind. I am lucky to have you as my final heir, in my decades of walking this earth alone, I met your mother. She was my light, till I lost her, she will always be my soul mate even when I take my last breath. Tell her that when she's ready to be good and when you old enough to be alpha, lead the clan better than I did, don't be like me. Love makes you weak. I became weak, but it never mattered because you became my strength, I love you my son, my Miyeon, My Park Miyeon. Carry my legacy wherever you go. Y/n, I love you, tears emitted from my eyes. I don't want this power anymore, it's killing me day by day. "We will find another way", Y/n hugs me not letting go..........................

Chapter 29

❝ I won't let you do this brother, you've hurt her enough, no more",
Tae pleads to me. Says you, anger starts building up in me. "Don't
Jimin, I'm so sorry okay for everything, but you hurting them", he looks
at him. Do I look like I care huh? "Yes you do care", he punches me
making me angrier. Ohh you shouldn't have done that. "I should have
someone who has to knock sense into you", he shoves and kicks me hard
making me fall. Get away from me Tae, I'm not the same, I can kill you
right here but I need you alive to take care of them. "I would like you
to see you try", he punches me hard making me bleed. Ohh is it, I spit
out the blood and stand but Y/n stands between us.

Y/n P.o.v

ENOUGH! I've had it with both of you, I'm tired of all this
fighting. Tae it's okay if wants then so be it. I'm sick and tired of
showing you Jimin, how I feel about you, you said I am yours and you
love me, but it doesn't feel so. I slap him so hard it hurt my heart. I gave
you a son, instead of being a man and fathering your son, who loves
you, by the way, you want to leave me with all this burden huh? HOW
DARE YOU PARK JIMIN HUH! Do what you want, and we leave,
I pull Miyeon and we leave, my whole body still shaking. "Mommy,
are you okay?" he asks. Yes baby, let's hope that stops your father if it
doesn't you know what to do. "I've never seen you like this", he spits
out blood. Are you okay Tae? "I'm a man Y/n I can take it, let's hope
we got through him", he looks at me hopefully. It was hard but it hurt

like hell but to save him, it felt right. "Mommy there's something else", Miyeon looks at Tae. What is it, baby? "Uncle Tae, take my blood, it will protect you from the power of the siren because she just arrived. " Y/n are you ok with this", he looks at me. Do it, just don't kill him or I will. He draws his blood. "I'm okay mommy see, don't worry", as he noticed pain in my eyes. You are my brave soldier, should we help Jimin? "He can take her, we there with him, she doesn't know that and neither does Jimin, for now, let's watch from afar at a distance, she can't smell us", Tae holds on to me. Oka, you look better. "It's his blood, it has healing powers which means if they find him, they will want him, gotta protect him Y/n no matter", he looks at me and I nod in approval.

Jimin P.o.v

Well, well look who decided to show up. "It's your bloody end boy, you think you're so damn powerful hahaha", she laughs. Watch it woman, who are you calling boy huh? "Are you even a man, you can't keep your woman, even your brothers have fucked her", she laughs. What has that got to do with you? "Everything because of that girl you have done your worst", she laughs as anger was overtaking me. Hahaha, I see what you doing, trying to manipulate me to self-doubt myself, and my power, too late she beat you to it. Why are you here old woman? "I will end you", she attacks making me fall, but I manage to stand up. Ok, end me, let's see what you got, she attacks again but I manage to stop her hard making her fall down. "Is that all you got huh?" she laughs. Without looking at me, she pushes a knife mixed with my blood knowing that was the only thing that could end Sirens, I pierced through her heart. That is what I got, now leave my family in peace, she takes her last breath and dies. My eyes manage to turn normal as I kneel before her. I'm tired of people attacking my family. "Hey, are you okay?" Jungkook comes near me. Yes, can you do something for me? "Yeah sure, what sup?" he looks worriedly at me. Call a clan meeting tonight, I want to address them. "Okay, you fine here?" he asks. Yes, he leaves.

Y/n P.o.v

Hey, Jimin are you okay? "Yeah I'm good", but he wasn't looking at me. "Hey Tae, take them home please", he pleads. "You should do that, you guys have to talk", he looks at Jimin. "No, there's nothing to talk about, please take care of them", he leaves. What's wrong with him now? "He'll come around, let's go home, it's not safe yet remember if they find out about Miyeon's power they will take him", Tae carries Miyeon and we leave for home.

Jimin P.o.v

I don't want her to see my monstrous side, I want her to choose me not Tae, but why would she choose a monster like me, I'm not worth it, I'm a father that's all that matters, I have to do right by him and never leave him. "Are you sure you okay?" Jungkook sits next to me. Do I look okay huh? "Never mind I asked, they waiting for you to address them", he looks at me. Thanks, let's go.

Y/n P.o.v

Hey Tae, where are you going? "Jimin called a meeting", he looks at me. You stay, I go, and I need answers. "No Y/n, all monsters will be there", he looks at me. Am I not one huh? No, you not, I kiss him locking my tongue with his. No Tae, I have to sort these issues between him, then I and you have to talk. "Okay then Y/n please be safe", he kisses me again. Keep my son safe at all costs, my life depends on it. "You know I will", he kisses me and I leave.

Jimin P.o.v

Kneel before you grand alpha, they all kneel. Anyone who is against my family and I leave now because if I find you myself, I will kill you, they all stay silent. I'm leaving Jungkook in charge for some time, as I train Miyeon to take over you as alpha, he will protect you. If you keep your word and I will kill you if you don't. "Are you sure Jimin," Jungkook looks at me? Yes, I have to sort my stuff, although I'm leaving you in charge, if you go back to your dark ways, I will end you this time. "I know you will, but I won't, sort yourself and sit on your throne and attend the vampire night, you know we can't miss that one", he smirks. Hahaha listen to you, I'll be there, talk to the clan, and I leave.

Y/n P.o.v

Why did he act like he didn't even care huh, I thought, tears falling. No Y/n you have to be strong to face him, I know where I'll find him, I get to the place but I fail to see him. I thought he loves me, but I feel his cold hands touching my waist. "Hey Luna", he kisses the back of my neck. For what exactly? "For making you wait, you thought I changed and all, I see it in your eyes but I haven't, not yet anyway, I don't want you to see my monstrous side", he looks at me. I'm not afraid of you Jimin. "You should be", he looks at me. Not when we love each other, I won't stand for this change you want to incline on the fact that if you say this I'll leave. Fuck that Jimin, I'm sick of it, I told you, I love you with that monstrous side, you have Miyeon, who idolizes everything you do, and don't you want to be with me? I turn and face him breathing close to him, don't I attract you anymore? Don't you see me as your woman anymore? I kiss him not letting go, he kisses me back pulling me close to him, and he lets go. " What makes you think I don't want you?, can't you see how attracted I am to you, how badly I want you if I didn't would I have made love to you knowing Tae was near huh?", he smirks. "Would I do this?" he kisses me deep, entailing his tongue with mine, as his hand traveled all around me making me quiver, wet and weak. Jimin I...... "Shhhh don't say anything, your body is doing all the talking", he smirks. I blush at the way I worshipped his touch, it made me weak. "I love you, Luna, don't ever doubt my love for you, you are my soulmate, our hearts are one, why do you question that huh? You are my Luna, whatever it takes", he smirks and kisses me deep making me wet as arousal was rising in me", he smirked again. Jimin I.... "Shh save this for after the event tonight, we need to talk with Tae he ain't gonna like that I took back what's mine", he kisses me again. You should never leave it. "I won't he kisses me again by now my lips were so swollen. We leave for a home together. "Daddy, you here", Miyeon runs up to him hugging him tightly. "Ohh someone is happy to see me", he smiles. "Yes daddy, I thought I lost you, I don't want you to leave me", he looks at him. "If I leave who will take of mommy huh?" he hugs him again. "No one daddy, not even me", he looks down. "Why not?" he asks. "That's your job, not mine", he smiles. "I forget how wise you are my son, daddy loves you never forget that my son, I want you to take over and be better than me", he smiles at him. "Hey Y/n, can we talk, seeing these two can't even notice us", he smiles at me. Okay let's go, you're right. Are you okay? "Yes I am, I'm sorry for everything", he hugs me. No, I should be sorry, I'm the one to blame for all this. " No Y/n, you didn't, I knew what I was doing, but I couldn't help it, greed took over me, how could I get in the way of what you and Jimin have, when it's so clear how good you look together, I won't leave you. I will always be with you no matter what, whenever you need me, and with Miyeon, he needs all the protection he can get but we have to tell Jimin", he smiles at me. "Tell me what?" he looks at us. It's about Miyeon. "What about him? Is he okay?" He looks at us worriedly. Yes, we just think people might want to harm him if they find out what he is capable of. "And what is that?" he looks at us. His blood can heal any wound and any bruise. "That would make him a target, we will protect him together brother", he smiles. "That's what I said", she's looking at us like we were crazy. Don't you guys have to go somewhere? "We do but we going with you", they smile. What about Miyeon? Lisa and Kai offered to watch him, I'll leave the pack in case the monsters come", he smiles. You already planned this, didn't you? "We couldn't help it, you worth everything, go change, we show you our world", they both smirk looking at me.

Chapter 30

Wow, there are so many people. "More like vampires", he smirks. Stop being smart on me. "I didn't do anything Luna, by the way, this dress looks so hot on you, pity it won't last on you that long", he smirks. See, you doing it again. "Hey Guys", Jungkook appears looking ravishingly hot. "Lookie who is wearing a suit tonight, I thought you don't do that ha-ha", Tae laughs. "I'm impressing ladies' man, what you think", he laughs. "That is a first for you, you look handsome", he smiles. "By the way, I have a surprise for you", he smirks. "Ok show me", Tae laughs. "Close your eyes", Jungkook pleads with Tae. "If I don't then what?" he looks at him. "You won't see your present, oops I mean surprise", he laughs. "Ayt, I'll play because I'm in a good mood", he closes his eyes. "Now open your eyes", he smiles. "Ohh my gosh, Rose, what? I mean you look good", he hugs her. Rose, now even I'm surprised too. Jimin why are you smiling like that? Did you have anything to do with this? "Maybe but it was Jungkook's idea, he believes these two need to talk and think about stuff", he smiles. You're right, let's go dance, me and you Rose we will catch up later. "Okay, I love you little sis", we leave.

Tae P.o.v

Hey, you look good. "Thank you, you too, I see Y/n and Jimin back together", she smiles. Yeah freakin soulmates, they belong together, and I'm sorry for everything but I'm not sorry for loving you. "Tae, I never stopped loving you", she smiled. Why? "Because I knew that it was never you", she looks at me. Thank you for tonight but tonight is about my brother, I wink at her.

Y/n P.o.v

Jimin you are so handsome. "I know, what else?" he smirks. You are sexy. "I know what else? He smirks. I love you. "How much?" he smirks. More than my life. "That's enough for me, you see I'm not so ancient", He smiles. You never have. He kisses me, what's wrong you are shaking. "It's cause I've never done this before", he looks down. Do what? He goes on one knee. Jimin what are you doing, emotions took over. "Over the years, I walked alone, till I saw you coming my way, I knew you were my soulmate, Y/n, I love you and I want to love you till my last, will you make me the happiest alpha, and be my wife, my queen alpha, and my eternal Luna", he looks at me. Yes to the first, yes to the second, and a big yes to the last. "Yes?" he checks. Yes, Jimin, I'll marry you, he stands, pressing his lips again with mine. "Save that for later geez, Tae smirks making me blush, Look at your cheeks turning red", Tae laughs. "Leave my wife to be alone", he smirks. "Congratulations you both", they hug. Thank you, so you knew, and didn't tell me. "Hahahaha bro code, I've never seen you glow like this", they laugh. "Congratulations you both, I will be the one to plan the wedding", he laughs. Hell No we both disagreed. "Okay at least let me dream it, geez you guys are killing my buzz", he laughs. We all enjoy the night, spending quality time with everyone. "Hie mommy and daddy", he smiles. Miyeon why do you look so happy? "Because you and daddy are going to be family", he smiles. "And who told you that?" Jimin smirks. "No one daddy, I saw it and felt it", he giggles. "That's my boy, I love you my son", Jimin picks him up. "I know daddy, can I go sleep with uncle Kai", he asks. It's okay baby, you look tired, kisses from both mommy and daddy, and he kisses me, that's my baby, goodnight. He says goodnight and leaves. "So that leaves me and you", he winks. Hahaha, you wish. "Is my wife to be already turning me down?" he looks at me. I am. "Hmm really, what about now?" he pulls me close to him. It's something, a knock disturbs us. "Who could be coming night, go be with Miyeon, we just have to be safe", he kisses me and leaves. As he opens the door, Miyeon screams, "No daddy, no, no, no, he cries, someone just stabbed daddy with Deadman's blood straight to the heart", he cries. My heart felt like it stopped as I ran to him. No, I can't lose you, not now baby, Miyeon stop crying mommy has to think. "Mommy, let's mix our blood, and we bring him back", he looks at me with his puffy eyes. What is his bad side comes? "He'll be alive mommy, if we don't he dies, it's killing him slowly, I can feel his pain", he cries. Okay, baby, we mix our blood and give it to Jimin but it doesn't work. "I don't know mommy", Miyeon winces in pain. "Why are you both crying, what happened, we heard his thoughts and cries, and came as fast as I could", Tae looked at Jimin worried. I gave him our blood it's not working. "That's odd", he looks at me. What do we do Tae? "Let's wait, it might work", he looks at Jimin worriedly. Five days pass still nothing, we've tried everything it's not working. "I know why, give him only Miyeon's blood, I'll explain if it works", Jungkook arrives running. We give him and he wakes up. Jungkook you did it, Jimin you came back to me as tears emitted from my eyes. "Thought I wasn't going to pull through, I could hear you but I was trapped", he smiles. Jungkook explain, please. "I talked with Suga, and he said the reason why the blood mixture wasn't working was that Y/n is pregnant and this time the baby is pure human. What? I felt like I had been caught. "Get this, she knows she's pregnant but didn't know she got a proper human", Jungkook smiles. "How is this possible?" Jimin asks looking shocked. "You never know", he laughs. I wanted to be sure, I look at Jimin. "I'm outta words Luna, you are my greatest gift, and now we are complete, Miyeon is getting a sibling, that's worth it Y/n, you are my forever soulmate, my Luna, mother of my heir and the queen alpha to my clan", he kisses me

......................................THE END..........................

Don't miss out!

Visit the website below and you can sign up to receive emails whenever CHANTELLE P NCUBE publishes a new book. There's no charge and no obligation.

https://books2read.com/r/B-A-PWNM-DJBZB

BOOKS 2 READ

Connecting independent readers to independent writers.

Also by CHANTELLE P NCUBE

Vampire's Lust

About the Author

My name is Chantelle Primrose Ncube. I was born in Zimbabwe, where I spent my early years. I am naturally an introvert, and I find serene peace when I am alone. My favorite color is cyan blue, yellow, turquoise blue and white. I love peace and quiet because it helps me gather my thoughts and makes me feel like I am breathing.

I grew up following BTS, they were my therapy when my mom and granddad passed away. I believe they helped me see my true potential. I was in a bad space, but when I listened to any BTS song I would find myself feeling at peace and happy. Wherever I go I'm always asked how I remain happy all the time even when I am going through a hard space and all I can say is thank you BTS. I also owe everything to my grandfather who raised me in books, he first introduced me to reading newspapers, and I was always drawn to mystical, supernatural and crime themes which led me to watching a lot of series that contained all that. As I wrote this book, I had a lot of thoughts as to how the boys would be if they were vampires not idols, and it got me flowing with this fantastic and mystical story.